ANGELIQUE WAS NO ANGEL

"Don't be angry with me for helping the Sioux break into the fort," Angelique said. "Those soldiers were no better than animals. I'm glad they're dead."

"Anything else you're glad about?" Skye Fargo asked.

"Yes," she said.

"And what might that be?"

"That you . . . don't have any clothes on under that blanket."

"After what you've been through," Skye said, "I thought you might have had enough of men."

She kept looking hard at him. "Enough of men? No, Fargo." And lifting the blanket, she joined him under it.

That morning, Angelique had been hungry for blood. Tonight she was hungry for something else. . . .

Exciting Westerns by Jon Sharpe

THE TRAILSMAN 42

RENEGADE COMMAND

by
Jon Sharpe

A SIGNET BOOK

NEW AMERICAN LIBRARY

PUBLISHER'S NOTE

This novel is a work of fiction. Names, characters, places, and incidents either are the product of the author's imagination or are used fictitiously, and any resemblance to actual persons, living or dead, events, or locales is entirely coincidental.

NAL BOOKS ARE AVAILABLE AT QUANTITY DISCOUNTS WHEN USED TO PROMOTE PRODUCTS OR SERVICES. FOR INFORMATION PLEASE WRITE TO PREMIUM MARKETING DIVISION, NEW AMERICAN LIBRARY, 1633 BROADWAY, NEW YORK, NEW YORK 10019.

The first chapter of this book previously appeared in *The Range Killers*, the forty-first volume in this series.

 SIGNET TRADEMARK REG. U.S. PAT. OFF. AND FOREIGN COUNTRIES
REGISTERED TRADEMARK—MARCA REGISTRADA
HECHO EN CHICAGO, U.S.A.

SIGNET, SIGNET CLASSIC, MENTOR, PLUME, MERIDIAN AND NAL BOOKS are published by New American Library, 1633 Broadway, New York, New York 10019

First Printing, June, 1985

1 2 3 4 5 6 7 8 9

PRINTED IN THE UNITED STATES OF AMERICA

The Trailsman

Beginnings . . . they bend the tree and they mark the man. Skye Fargo was born when he was eighteen. Terror was his midwife, vengeance his first cry. Killing spawned Skye Fargo, ruthless, cold-blooded murder. Out of the acrid smoke of gunpowder still hanging in the air, he rose, cried out a promise never forgotten.

The Trailsman, they began to call him, all across the West: searcher, scout, hunter, the man who could see where others only looked, his skills for hire but not his soul, the man who lived each day to the fullest, yet trailed each tomorrow. Skye Fargo, the Trailsman, the seeker who could take the wildness of a land and the wanting of a woman and make them his own.

*1861—Sioux country, where Fargo finds
himself caught between a Sioux chieftain's fury
and the treacherous troopers of his renegade command.*

1

At first glance the fort below—Fort Alexander—
looked perfectly normal. As Fargo forked his powerful black-and-white Ovaro—the hot July sun
resting like a welome hand on his shoulder—his
keen eyes took in the ragged palisades and log
quarters, the dusty parade ground, and the low
profile of the sutler's store. Fargo was pleased.
Before this night was out he would be sleeping
under army blankets, and more than likely, this
would come after he and the major had plundered
his reserves of bourbon.

But an instant later the Trailsman's sharp eyes
caught something that caused him to frown with
sudden concern. A troop of cavalry was riding
through the fort's gates without challenge.
Watching them dismount in front of their barracks, Fargo could not help noticing their ragged,
careless bearing. Some were not wearing their

campaign hats and others had failed to put on their cavalry tunics, their broad yellow braces standing out clearly against their underwear.

Fargo's uneasiness grew more pronounced when he noted also the absence of brisk, purposeful activity about the fort and the lack of horseflesh standing at the hitch rack in front of the sutler's store. No women were visible, and on the clotheslines behind the enlisted men's quarters, not a single stitch of clothing was hanging in the hot sun.

Fargo spurred the pinto on down the slope. Despite his size, the powerful Ovaro carried him with deceptive ease. Dressed in a buckskin shirt, jacket, and pants and wearing a wide-brimmed hat, Fargo was a big, broad-shouldered man with hair as black as a raven's wing, a sharp, powerful blade of a nose, eyes the color of a lake under a blue sky.

It had not rained in weeks and the tall grass was scorched yellow, the trees drooping listlessly in the windless, ovenlike heat. But Fargo was not thinking of the weather at the moment. He was wondering what had happened to Maj. Hollister's command. Fargo knew the major as a no-nonsense, spit-and-polish disciplinarian fresh out of West Point and a strategist who was already a match for the local Sioux chieftain, Black Feather.

The only thing Fargo could figure was that something must have happened to the major.

Fargo gained the flat and headed for the entrance to the fort. Unlike so many army posts in the West—which were usually a careless sprawl of buildings set out on a flat with little or no barrier to the hostiles—Fort Alexander was surrounded by a log palisade. It had been called Fort Henry in the days of the American Fur Company, and the fur company builders, anxious to protect their stores of beaver, bear, and buffalo hides, had taken advantage of the heavily timbered slopes surrounding the fort to build the barricade.

Ahead of Fargo the fort's gates sagged open. There was no sentry in sight and Fargo was not challenged as he rode through the gates and into the fort. He pulled his pinto up and looked around. The few troopers he saw watched him warily, and not one greeted him cordially. Across the parade ground one trooper hurried into the headquarters building, glancing quickly back at Fargo just before he disappeared.

Fargo nudged the pinto forward, and before he finished crossing the parade ground, what appeared to be the C.O. and two other troopers stepped from the headquarters building and halted on the low porch to wait for him. When Fargo reached them, he noticed that the commanding officer was a captain: a pale, slack-jawed soldier with watery eyes and sandy hair. He needed a shave and his uniform was in even worse disrepair than that of his sergeant.

Fargo pulled up and dismounted.

"My name's Skye Fargo," he told the captain, dropping the pinto's reins over the hitch rail. "Where's Major Hollister?"

"He pulled out."

"Pulled out?"

"There's a war on back East. Or ain't you heard."

"I heard, Captain."

"So we're all that's left to keep the peace hereabouts." The captain smiled coldly. "I'm Captain Edward Blaine. You're welcome to stay the night."

"Thank you, Captain."

"What's your business in the area, Fargo? This ain't very friendly country. Black Feather's band has gone loco."

"I'm looking for a man—maybe two men—last seen headed this way."

"You a bounty hunter?"

"No. I just want the man."

"You don't care about any bounty?"

"Nope."

"Well, outside of a few settlers passing through, you're the first stranger my men and I have seen in weeks. You won't find them two you're lookin' for in this fort."

"Wasn't expectin' I would." Fargo glanced over at the sutler's store. It looked deserted and Fargo had been looking forward to wetting his whistle. "Did the sutler pull out with the major?"

Captain Blaine nodded.

"I'm sure sorry to hear that. I'm dry as sawdust."

"A word of advice," Captain Blaine told him. "The store is boarded up for a reason. Stay away from it. Everything in there's army property—including the rum."

"I'm not a thief, Captain."

"Just so we understand each other."

Capt. Blaine turned to his sergeant. "Take Mister Fargo's horse to the stable, Sergeant, then show him to his quarters."

The captain turned and walked back inside the headquarters building. Leading his pinto, Fargo followed the sergeant across the compound to the stables.

After Fargo had seen to the pinto, the big, red-faced noncom escorted him from the stables, then led him to the officers' quarters, a series of low mud-and-log buildings.

Fargo stepped into a cheerless room furnished only with a broken chest of drawers and a single dusty army cot.

Turning to the sergeant, Fargo said, "Tell me, Sergeant. What do you think of the captain?"

The sergeant eyed Fargo warily. "What do you mean?"

"From the look of this post, he's a damn slack commanding officer."

"We like him just fine."

"Do you, now?"

"Maybe you'd do better to keep your opinions to yourself around here, mister."

"That a threat, Sergeant?"

"Take it any way you like."

"I'll do that, Sergeant."

The sergeant turned and left. Stepping to the door, Fargo watched the sergeant walk back to headquarters. The big fellow slouched. His hat was perched precariously on the back of his head. His shirt, filthy, he kept open at the collar.

Fargo looked away from the sergeant and studied the other troopers who were moving listlessly about the compound. They were no better dressed and walked with no more pride or discipline than did their sergeant or commanding officer.

These soldiers did not impress Fargo, not one damn bit. And he had no confidence in this command's ability to offer protection for any settlers passing through. And as for keeping Black Feather and his Sioux in line, these sorry excuses for the U.S. cavalry would be pretty near helpless.

Fargo decided he'd better push on first thing in the morning. This fort reminded him of a house of cards waiting to collapse.

Stowing his gear under the cot a moment later, Fargo heard the rumble of wagon wheels and the high, nervous whinny of horses being driven close to their limit. He glanced out the window and saw two wagons charging through the gate into the fort—a tall, dark-haired woman handling the first team, a grizzled old timer vaguely familiar to Fargo driving the second team. The old-timer's wagon had its canvas top burned through in spots and a large torn piece of it was flapping in the wind like a broken wing. It was obvious what was up. The wagons were fleeing from hostiles—Black Feather, more than likely.

As the wagons rattled to a halt, two troopers ran over belatedly to pull the gate shut, while other troopers—including the captain and his sergeant—hurried out of the headquarters building and started across the parade ground. Fargo stepped out of his quarters and watched the bearded fellow driving the second wagon jump to the ground to help the woman down from her wagon.

That was all it took. At once Fargo recognized the old-timer. He was Jeb Dugan!

Pleased, Fargo hurried out to greet his old friend. Jeb had aged considerably these past ten years; it was his white head and white beard that had momentarily confounded Fargo. But there was no mistaking the easy way the big trapper carried his still-powerful, heavily muscled body.

"Jeb, you son of a bitch," Fargo cried, brushing past the captain to shake the old-timer's hand.

"Fargo," Jeb cried as he grabbed Fargo's hand and pumped it heartily. "What in blazes're you doin' here?"

"Just rode in."

Jeb sobered then. "You still lookin' for them four varmints?"

"Reckon so."

"You gettin' any closer."

"There's only two left now."

"Well, now," Jeb said by way of comment. Then he turned to the girl standing beside him. "This here's Skye Fargo, Theresa," he told her. Then he looked back at Fargo. "Meet Theresa Wayland, Fargo."

Fargo touched the brim of his hat to the woman. She returned his greeting with a tight, barely perceptible nod. It was clear she was close to collapse after all she had been through. Fargo glimpsed a dismal, naked despair in her eyes.

"Just got through snatching Theresa away from Black Feather," Jeb explained. "Wasn't so lucky with the others, though. And them redskins've still got my pack horses and pelts."

"Would you like to explain what happened, mister?" the captain asked, stepping closer. It was clear he was irritated at the way Jeb had left off his account the moment Fargo joined them.

"Sure, Captain," Jeb said. "Like I was sayin', Black Feather and his braves were chasing after me for my skins when they came onto these two wagons. They left me for the wagons, but I managed to snatch them back when I stole Miss Wayland from their camp."

"What happened to the other settlers?" Fargo asked.

Theresa spoke up then. "My father was taken captive. So was the family in the other wagon."

"How many in that other party?"

"A man and wife," said Jeb. "And two young' uns."

"How old were the kids?"

"The boy was eight, the girl six."

Fargo frowned. He did not like the sound of that.

"You know what happened to the family?" the captain asked.

"We ain't sure," Jeb said. "Last I heard, the husband was hollerin' somethin' fearful. Them Sioux didn't take kindly to the way he shot up the attackin' war party."

"Did Black Feather follow you here?" the captain asked Jeb.

"They was on my shirttail last time I looked."

The captain's face went pale. He turned and began issuing orders to the sergeant, who seemed close to panic as he ran off to alert the post.

The captain turned to Theresa. "If you will allow me, Miss Wayland, I'll escort you to your quarters. I warn you, though, they ain't much."

"That's all right," Theresa said. "I'll stay here—in my wagon. There's my bed inside and most of my belongings."

"As you wish." The captain stalked off.

"Well, now," said Jeb, watching Blaine depart. "Ain't *he* a friendly cuss."

"No, he ain't, and that's the pure truth of it."

"If you'll excuse me, gentlemen," said Theresa. "I find I am exhausted." She turned then and clambered wearily up into her wagon.

"Don't you worry none about that black-hearted Injun chief, Miss Wayland," Jeb told her. "You're safe now. We'll all see to that."

"Thank you," she managed, disappearing into her wagon.

A moment later, as Fargo and Jed started to move off, they heard a muffled sound coming from within the wagon and realized it was the woman's sobs as Theresa Wayland, contemplating the miserable fate of her father and those she had traveled with these long months past, was finally venting her despair.

*　　*　　*

Not long after, Black Feather and a small band

of Sioux appeared at the far end of the flat. The alarm was sounded, not by a bugler but by a series of shouts. As Fargo and Jeb watched from Fargo's room, men rushed to post themselves near the gate while others mounted the rickety catwalks that ran along the tops of the palisades. Still a rag-tag, uninspiring lot, they were moving now with some urgency. The threat of hostiles had a way of making even the most lackadaisical troops concentrate powerfully on the business at hand.

Fargo and Jeb stepped outside and hastened across the compound. Fargo lugging his Sharps and Jeb his Hawken, they climbed up the ladders to the scaffold and took their places beside the troopers. But when the Sioux saw where the wagons' tracks led, they pulled up. After a short parley, the chief raised his rifle in a gesture of defiance, then wheeled his pony and disappeared into the timber. The rest of his braves let loose with a few piercing war cries and followed after him.

In only a few moments, the threat had passed.

Giddy with relief, the troopers streamed back down the ladders and immediately lapsed into their former disorderly state. Laughing in relief and digging one another with their elbows, they trailed off to their barracks, some of them already unsteady on their feet as they pulled on the flasks of whiskey they hauled out of their back pockets.

Watching them reel off, Fargo shook his head. "I don't like it," he told Jeb as he watched the troopers.

"Yeah. I been watching, too. This is sure as hell one slack army post."

"I just hope Black Feather doesn't come back. Before long, these troopers will be so sloshed, they won't be able to hit the ground with their hats."

"They ain't a pretty bunch, and that's a fact. But I'm mighty grateful for them all the same."

"Why?"

"Because they got this fort open and fully manned. That wasn't supposed to be. If it hadn't a been open and manned, them Sioux would be drying out my scalp along about now."

At Jeb's words, Fargo halted and turned to face him. "What do you mean, Jeb? Wasn't this fort *supposed* to be manned?"

"No, it wasn't."

"How come?"

"The word I got from Fort Platte was Major Hollister had done pulled out his entire command, on account of that there unpleasantness back East, something called the War Between the States." Jeb shook his head. "I don't mind telling you. I'm sure as hell grateful the army changed its mind and left this detachment behind."

Fargo resumed walking. "Maybe the army didn't change its mind, Jeb."

"Now, what in tarnation do you mean by that?"

"Jeb, I don't think the army had a thing to do with these men being here—or assigning Captain Blaine as their commanding officer. Hell, to begin with, I don't even think Blaine *is* an officer."

"You serious, Fargo?"

"Hell, look at the man. You noticed his manners right off."

"Jesus, Fargo. Do you know what you're sayin'?"

They entered Fargo's quarters. Fargo closed the door, went to the window, and peered out across the compound, his eyes on the headquarters building.

"Sure, I know what I'm saying," Fargo replied. "These here ain't regular troops. They're deserters, renegades. As soon as the major pulled out, they moved into the post and took it over."

Jeb scratched his head meditatively. "I got to admit you got the captain pegged. He sure as hell don't look or act like no officer I ever seen. An' he sure as hell keeps a mean and sloppy post. But supposin' you're right? How're we goin' to find out for sure?"

"A little while ago," Fargo replied, "the captain warned me away from the sutler's store. Soon's it gets dark enough—say around midnight—maybe you and I better go find out why."

"You're on, Fargo."

The board groaned as Fargo bent it back, pulling the carelessly hammered nails out with it. With a sudden crack, it broke free. Jeb got a firm grip on the second board and pulled that out as well, giving them access to the store's narrow back door. Fargo tried the knob, but the door was locked.

"Stand back," whispered Jeb.

The big trapper placed his right foot on the door, just under the knob, and thrust forward.

The lock held, but the doorjamb splintered and the door sagged open.

The two men moved cautiously into the sutler's store. Fargo found a lantern and lit it. They came to a storeroom and pulled up just outside it.

"Oh, bloody Jesus," Jeb exclaimed. "What's that smell?"

"Someone's in there," Fargo agreed. "But he's sure as hell ripe."

Holding handkerchiefs over their faces, the two men pushed open the door to the storeroom, then turned away, hardly able to keep their stomachs from heaving up their contents. There was a big, redheaded man in his fifties lying on the floor. Holding the lantern over the still body, Fargo saw the dead man's bloodstained apron still tied about his waist and knew at once who it was.

The sutler hadn't left with the major, after all.

"What's that?"

Both men pulled back and listened. A steady, agitated thumping was coming from the other side of the store. It resembled the sound a boot or shoe would make if it were kicking continually at a wall or door.

"Close off the storeroom," Fargo told Jeb as he hurried into the front of the store, skirted the counter, and headed for another door leading to the granery. Holding the lantern high with one hand, he pulled the door open and found himself looking down at the disheveled, bound-and-gagged figure of a young woman. Her dress was torn from ankle to hip, and her blouse had been ripped off her shoulders. She was close to being naked, and he could see that her pale figure was covered with bruises. Putting the lantern down beside her, Fargo untied the gag. Tears of frustration and rage coursed down her face.

"Who are you?" she panted, her eyes flashing with fury. "You don't look like troopers."

"We ain't."

"Please! Don't let that bastard near me again!"

"Who do you mean?" Jeb asked.

"The captain."

"Easy, now, easy," said Fargo, taking out his bowie and slicing through the rope that bound her ankles and wrists. "We ain't goin' to let anyone near you if you don't want."

Behind them, the front door slammed open. Fargo spun to see the sergeant pause in the doorway. The large navy Colt in his hand was cocked and there was a pleased grin on his face as he leveled the muzzle on Fargo and tightened his finger on the trigger.

Fargo still had the bowie in his hand. In one single powerful upward stroke, he flung it at the sergeant. The knife left his palm on a flat trajectory and sliced into the man's chest, the long blade slipping neatly between his ribs to bury itself hilt deep into his heart. With only a slight, barely audible gasp, the sergeant sagged to the floor, plunging forward onto the knife, driving its blade in still deeper.

Jeb hurried to the sergeant's side and flung him over.

"He's a gone beaver," Jeb told Fargo, pulling the knife free.

Fargo took the knife from Jeb and looked back at the girl. Her face was a stark white as she stared wide-eyed at the dead man. Then she looked at Fargo, the color rushing back into her face. "You killed him!"

"I had no choice."

"You think I care? He was going to take me to the captain."

"That means Blaine is waiting for you now."

"Yes."

"And where would he be waitin'?"

"In the headquarters building. He sleeps in his office."

"Maybe it's time I gave the captain a visit," Fargo told Jeb. Then he looked back at the girl. "What's your name?"

"Angelique. My father runs this store."

Fargo winced inwardly and glanced up at Jeb.

Angelique pushed herself to a sitting position. In her state she was unaware of how scantily she was clad and of its possible effect on Fargo or Jeb.

"Have you seen my father?" the girl asked anxiously. "He's a big man with red hair. He must be worried about me. I must go to him."

Without replying to her, Fargo looked quickly up at Jeb. "Take care of Angelique," he said. "I want a chat with this captain."

"You sure you won't need me?"

"I'd rather you stay with Angelique. It might not be a bad idea if you took her to Miss Wayland's wagon."

"Good idea," Jeb said, helping the girl to her feet.

As Jeb and the girl slipped out into the darkness, Fargo wiped off his bowie's blade and cut back out through the rear of the store.

There was a thin sliver of light visible under the door to the captain's office. Fargo knocked once, softly.

"That you, Sergeant?"

Fargo mumbled something.

Footsteps approached the door, and a second later it was pulled open. Fargo pushed into the dim room, the muzzle of his Colt thrusting deep into the captain's soft belly.

"Angelique ain't comin' tonight," said Fargo.

"Why, how did you know?"

Then the captain caught himself and took a step back. Fargo followed him and slammed the door shut behind him.

The captain, dressed only in his filthy long johns, looked desperately around for his weapon—a Colt resting on his desk.

Fargo stepped past him, snatched it up, and thrust it into his belt. "Now, suppose you explain what's going on here," Fargo told Blaine, shoving him into the chair behind his desk.

"I don't have to explain nothin' to you," Blaine said defiantly. "You can't touch me. Fire that gun and my men will be in here before you holster your weapon. You're my prisoner—you and that old mountain man. Black Feather's waitin' for you outside the fort, and my men have you inside." He reached out for Fargo's gun. "You better let me have that."

Fargo slammed the barrel hard against the side

of Blaine's face. The force of the blow nearly lifted the man from his chair. His hand held dazedly up to his left cheekbone, he looked with sullen, watery eyes up at Fargo.

"We found the sutler," Fargo told him.

Blaine swallowed, but made no effort to explain.

"You killed him. Why?"

"He tried to kill me."

"He must have had a good reason."

Blaine laughed shortly, contemptuously. "He didn't want me to take his daughter. He said she was too good for me."

"From the looks of it, she is."

Still holding his rapidly swelling chin, Blaine stormed, "I could've had you killed soon's you rode in here. But I let you live. So you owe me. Now, put down that gun if you want to ride out of here alive."

"Maybe I can't get out of here alive if you sic your men on me. But you won't make it out alive either."

"Damn you! What do you want?"

"For starters, how many men you got?"

"Thirty-two."

"All of them deserters?"

"Most of them," Blaine admitted.

"And the rest?"

Blaine grinned. "I rescued them from the guardhouse."

"But they're troopers, every one of them."

"That's right."

"Good."

Blaine frowned. "What're you plannin', mister?"

"Stand up, Blaine."

"What for?"

"Do like I tell you."

Slowly, warily, Blaine got to his feet.

"Turn around."

"Damn you, Fargo," the man cried, too terrified to budge. "What are you going to do?"

Fargo grabbed Blaine's shoulder and spun him around. Then he slammed the barrel of his Colt down onto Blaine's head. The man grunted slightly and sagged sideways. Catching Blaine before he fell to the floor, Fargo slung the unconscious man over his shoulder and hurried from the office.

A moment later, still carrying Blaine, Fargo moved swiftly across the dark parade ground toward the wagons barely visible ahead of him. He and Jeb still had much to do before this night was out, and if they were successful, they would find themselves with the lovely task of taking over and hammering into shape this renegade command of murderers, malingerers, and deserters.

A wild scheme maybe, but it was the only way Fargo could think of to get the hell out of there still wearing his scalp, and just maybe get those two kids and the rest of the settlers out of Black Feather's clutches.

2

Jeb Dugan poked his head out of the second wagon, the one with the burnt holes and the big flapping tear in the canvas. Angelique stuck her head out also.

"Give me a hand," Fargo told Jeb.

Jeb jumped to the ground and together they slung the unconscious man up into the wagon. He landed on the wagon bed with a succession of dull thuds. Fargo and Jeb clambered up into the wagon and pulled the tattered canvas cover up more securely over the bows. Jeb lit an oil lamp. Blaine was lying on his side, still unconscious, one arm outflung. Angelique stepped back and away from the captain, staring down at him with obvious loathing, her eyes blazing with fury.

Fargo assumed Jeb had already told her of her father's death, and she was undoubtedly thinking of that now as she stared down at Blaine. For a moment Fargo wondered if Angelique would be able to hold back her fury. He was glad she was not holding a weapon. Suddenly she lashed out with her foot, her boot catching Blaine on the side of his head. Blaine groaned softly, then lay still, a thin trickle of blood coming from the broken flesh over his temple.

Fargo reached out and took Angelique's arm. "I know how you feel," he told her.

"Do you?"

Fargo smiled bleakly. "All right. Maybe I don't. But that's enough, don't you think?"

She looked away. "For now maybe."

Jeb glanced up from Blaine and over to Fargo. "What now?" he asked.

"Tie him and gag him," Fargo said. "Securely."

"Fine. Then what?"

"We disarm the rest of these here troopers."

"They may not stand still for that."

"So we'll just have to make them."

Jeb grinned. "Well, now, that shouldn't be no tougher than ropin' a buffalo with a fishnet."

Fargo nodded. "Hell, it might even be as interestin'."

"When do you want to start?"

"Now."

"I'll tie up Blaine," said Angelique. "You two go ahead."

Fargo glanced at her. She seemed to have calmed down some. "Thanks."

As Angelique grabbed a length of rope, Jeb reached over to the corner of the wagon where he had stashed his Hawken. For a second he hefted it, then put it back. Watching him, Fargo nodded in agreement. The two of them would be working in close quarters. Jeb's knife and his huge Walker Colt would have to do.

"Ready?" Fargo asked.

Jeb nodded.

As they dropped lightly to the ground and started away from the wagons, Theresa Wayland looked out of her wagon, her pale face revealing her concern.

"Mister Fargo," she whispered, "I'm certain I just saw you carry an unconscious man to the other wagon. It looked like the captain."

"That's who is was, ma'am."

"Mister Fargo! What on earth is going on?"

"There's no time to explain that now. I suggest you join Angelique Santez in the other wagon. She'll be glad to explain."

He left her then and hurried off with Jeb across the dark ground toward the barracks.

Fargo and Jeb stood in the corner just inside the door, waiting for their eyes to get adjusted to the gloom. The barracks stank. The floor was littered with shirts and britches and bottles. Most of the troopers sprawled facedown on their cots, fully clothed. There were seventeen men in all. To make sure, Fargo and Jeb counted twice.

The troopers' rifles were leaning against the walls near their cots. Fargo and Jeb spent a ticklish time carefully taking them outside the barracks. A quick inspection showed that more than a few of the rifles had lost their firing pins or were so gummed up that they looked practically useless.

Now it was time for the hard part.

Even in the dim light, the two men could clearly see the holsters and handguns under the individual cots or hanging from gunbelts close by their heads. Disarming each individual trooper while he slept would not be easy. But they had no alternative.

They were almost done and Fargo was leaning over a trooper, in the act of removing a Colt from his holster, when the trooper stirred, rolled over, and looked up at Fargo.

He opened his mouth. Fargo's hand closed about his throat, his fingers tightening like steel cords. Then he smiled down at the trooper and shook his head slowly. The man stopped struggling. Fargo released his neck, unholstered his Colt, and with a quick, sharp crack knocked the man unconscious.

Across the aisle, Jeb was stepping away from a cot, a revolver in his hand. As Fargo glanced over at Jeb, he saw the trooper Jeb had just disarmed sit bolt upright in his cot.

"Hey!" the trooper cried. "What the hell?"

Stealth was no longer needed. Fargo fired his Colt into the ceiling. The barracks exploded with voices. Stepping away from the cots, their backs to opposite walls, both men leveled their weapons on the confused men.

"Stay right where you are," Fargo barked. "All of you."

The barracks quieted and Fargo peered carefully at the dark, shadowed figures crouching warily on their cots.

To a trooper close beside him, Fargo said, "Light a lamp."

The trooper did as he was bid, and in a moment there was enough light, fitful though it was, for Fargo and Jeb to see the troopers.

There were only six left who were still armed.

"Kick your weapons over here," Fargo told them.

"And do it easy-like," cautioned Jeb.

The men grumbled some but did as they were told.

While Fargo covered the men, Jeb bent to pick up the revolvers that went skidding over the floor to them. Fargo stopped one sidearm with his foot, bent, and stuck it into his belt. Jeb, his arms full, ducked outside to dump the handguns alongside the rifles.

"Now, get up," Fargo told the men, "all of you, and turn around."

"What're you gonna do?" one of the men asked fearfully.

"Never mind that. Just do as I say."

Reluctantly, the troopers got off their cots and turned their backs on Fargo and Jeb.

"Now march over to the other wall."

As they shuffled unhappily forward, Fargo stepped cautiously after them. A sound close on his heels alerted him. He swung around. The trooper he had clubbed earlier was on his feet.

Before Fargo could raise his Colt, the trooper flung himself on Fargo, dragging him down heavily, the back of his head crunching onto the floor. He was dimly aware of the other troopers spinning around. As the trooper reached over and grabbed for the gun in Fargo's belt, Fargo twisted his own Colt up and fired into the man's chest. The round knocked him back on his heels, his eyes wide in terror as he looked down at the hole in his filthy undershirt.

Ignoring him, Fargo spun about to cover the others, but two more troopers were already lunging toward him. Before Fargo could cock his Colt, Jeb darted back into the barracks and blasted both troopers with his big Walker. The nearest trooper spun to the floor, a hole in his shattered thigh. The other one grabbed at his right shoulder as he was flung back.

The other troopers moved quickly back.

Fargo got to his feet. "You two," he said, pointing with his gun, "see to those wounded men."

As the two men dragged the wounded troopers over to a cot, Jeb hurried over to join Fargo. "You all right?" he wanted to know.

"Sure. I'm feelin' a little silly, that's all."

"Hang in there. So far we're ahead of them."

"We hope so." Fargo turned to the troopers and ordered them to sit on the floor. Grumbling, they did as Fargo directed.

"Now, then, listen," Fargo told them. "And listen good. We've got Blaine in one of the wagons and the sergeant is dead."

There was a dim mutter from the troopers at this.

Fargo ignored it. "The thing is," he went on,

"we're in the middle of hostile country. So even if you don't like it, you're goin' to have to finally act like troopers."

"Yeah?" said one. "What makes you so sure of that?"

"I'm sure because you won't have any choice in the matter."

Another trooper smiled. His face was swarthy, unshaven, his dark, liquid eyes calculating. "I tell you what," he said. "Give us our guns back and we'll just see about that."

Fargo walked over to the man, cocked his Colt, aimed at a spot between his eyes, lifted the muzzle a fraction, and squeezed the trigger. The awful detonation shattered the barracks as the bullet seared a path through the man's thick shock of black hair.

Glaring up at Fargo, the trooper gingerly patted his newly parted hair. Then he looked at his hand. It came away bloody. But the trooper's defiance remained, if just a mite subdued.

"That's what I like," said Fargo to the rest of the troopers. "Someone to give me an excuse to show you I mean what I say."

"Give us time, you bastard," a trooper in back muttered.

Ignoring the remark, Fargo told them to get some sleep, promising a busy day ahead of them. He asked if anyone could play a bugle, but there was no response as the surly troopers simply stared back at Fargo.

Meeting their chill gaze, Fargo had no difficulty

33

at all reading their minds. Hell would freeze over before they would cooperate with him.

"Okay," said Fargo. "I'll use a gunshot to wake you."

When morning came, Fargo did not need his gun to awaken the men. They appeared outside the barracks just as dawn broke, a mean, restless crowd of angry men, staring across the parade ground at the two wagons.

The night before Fargo and Jeb—with the aid of a few sullen conscripts—had stored the confiscated weapons and ammunition in the wagon Jeb had taken. Angelique Santez, alert the moment they appeared beside the wagons, offered at once to stand guard over the armory—on the condition that she be issued a loaded rifle.

Fargo agreed at once. In a pinch he would rely on her as readily as he would Jeb. A woman who had suffered cruelly at these troopers' hands, she was angrier than a nest of yellow jackets and was clearly anxious for any excuse to pay them back. Theresa Wayland, though she did not offer to help in that fashion, had stuck close by Angelique throughout the night, in order to offer the angry, beaten woman some comfort.

Both men had taken turns sleeping, managing to snatch close to four hours' sleep between them. It was a chancy, nerve-racking slumber that Jeb compared to a pilgrim with his hands clamped around the tail of a rattlesnake: since he couldn't let go, he had to keep snapping the damn snake's head out in front of him.

The only question was how long Fargo and Jeb could keep snapping the rattlesnake's head.

As soon as the troopers appeared, the two men left the wagons and walked over to them. The troopers had made no effort to dress in full uniform or line up in any kind of formation. The playacting was over as far as they were concerned.

"The wounded men," Fargo said, pulling up in front of the troopers. "How are they?"

"Dead," the first of Fargo's "volunteers" told him.

"All of them?"

"Yeah."

"Have you buried them?"

The man nodded.

"When?"

"Last night."

"Where?"

There was a sudden bark of ugly laughter when the reply came: "In the outhouse behind the officers' quarters."

Fargo looked at Jeb. Two of the three men had not been that badly hurt. Fargo did not believe what the men were telling him and he could see Jeb did not believe them either. Fargo looked back at the troopers and pointed to the one whose hair he had parted the night before, the swarthy one.

"What's your name?"

"Alvarez."

"I think you and the rest are full of shit, Alvarez."

"You don't believe us, come see for yourself."

"I'll be right back," Fargo said to Jeb. Then, to Alvarez he said, "Lead the way."

They had almost reached the corner of the barracks. Alvarez was a couple of steps ahead of him when two sharp, electrifying screams came from the wagons. Fargo spun around. Immediately Alvarez jumped at Fargo and caught him from behind, his forearm slamming down over his face and closing upon his Adam's apple. Fargo stepped back, then reached behind Alvarez and grabbed his shirt. Ducking his head, he flung Alvarez to the ground. As soon as the man hit, Fargo lashed out with the toe of his boot, catching Alvarez on the side of the jaw. His head snapped back and he lay still.

Jeb was running toward the wagons, the troopers streaming after him. Fargo cocked his Colt and fired a warning shot over their heads. They scrambled hastily to a halt. One trooper, however, darted for cover behind the far corner of the mess hall. Fargo snapped off a quick shot and caught him in the small of the back. One less rattlesnake to worry about.

Fargo raced after Jeb. They were both almost to the wagons when one of the troopers Fargo had wounded in the thigh the night before tumbled backward out through the second wagon's torn canvas. Angelique leapt to the ground beside the dazed trooper and proceeded to kick the man about the head and shoulders furiously.

Inside the wagon Theresa Wayland could be heard struggling with another trooper. Jeb climbed into the wagon with surprising swiftness and agility for a man his age, and a moment later he flung the second trooper from the wagon. The trooper hit heavily, but was up in an instant. Fargo stepped close to him and sent him back down again with a tremendous punch to his jaw. Jumping down beside Fargo, Jeb finished the trooper off with a single kick to his head.

Fargo pulled Angelique off the other trooper. The man had been punished enough. His face and head were a bloody mess. When Jeb dragged the other one over and dumped him beside the one Angelique had finished off, Fargo recognized him as the fellow Fargo had nicked high in the shoulder the night before.

The troopers' plan had been to lull Fargo and Jeb into thinking these two were dead, giving them the opportunity to raid the wagons and retrieve their weapons. The troopers had not counted on Angelique or Theresa Wayland.

Fargo and Jeb looked back at the troopers. They had halted about twenty yards away from the two wagons. In front of the barracks, the sprawled figure of Alvarez was visible, and beyond him, the body of the man Fargo had shot in the back.

Fargo pointed to one of the troopers, a squat, dusty-looking fellow. "What's your name?"

"Tyler."

"Form a detail and take these two back to your barracks. And this time see to it that you do bury your dead."

As Tyler and the two men he selected helped the two groggy men to their feet, Fargo looked over the rest of the men. They shifted uncomfortably under his gaze, and Fargo began to hope they were beginning to accept the situation.

"Which one of you is the cook?"

They looked in amazement at one another. There had not been any effort by the captain to set up a mess, it seemed. They were left to shift for themselves, cooking their own meals, when and if they felt like it.

"All right, then. I'm going to appoint a cook," Fargo told them, "unless you want to pick someone."

They all looked at one long, lean, string bean of a fellow with watery eyes and a trembling chin.

Fargo looked directly at him. "Can you cook?"

The trooper nodded unhappily. "Yessir."

"What's your name?"

"The men, they all used to call me Cookie, sir. Before I lit out, that is."

"You mean deserted."

"Yessir."

"Well, then, Cookie, you're it. I'm putting you in charge of the mess in this fort. Open up that cook shack over there and take what you need from the sutler's store. And choose whoever you want to help."

Cookie quickly selected three troopers and started back to the mess hall with them.

Watching them go, Jeb stepped up beside Fargo and spoke to him softly. "Don't forget the sutler's body. It's still in the store."

Fargo nodded grimly. "Cookie!"

The man turned back around, his huge Adam's apple bobbing as he swallowed.

"The sutler's body is inside the storeroom. Revive Alvaraz and have him bury it."

"Alvarez?"

"You heard me."

Cookie turned back around again. Then Fargo told the rest of the troopers to clean their barracks and get ready for an inspection. They were incredulous, but one look at Fargo's hard eyes and they turned back around and shuffled off toward the barracks.

"You crazy?" asked Jeb.

"We got to keep them busy," Fargo explained. "And off our backs. You got any better ideas?"

Jeb chuckled and looked after the dispirited men. "Nope."

Cookie turned out to be a magician. Late though the breakfast was, it was a good one, and the troopers crowding into the mess hall could not hide their pleasure at the hot meal of beans, salt pork and bacon, fresh hardtack—and the abundance of hot coffee. Fargo and a sullen and battered Capt. Blaine, escorted by Jeb, joined the men in the mess, sitting at a smaller table reserved for the officers.

Finishing up his coffee, Fargo looked over the men. "I want five volunteers."

"For what?" a trooper asked.

"The Sioux captured some white settlers—two small kids among them—and we're gonna rescue them."

"You must be crazy," one trooper said.

"You've just volunteered."

Then Fargo pointed at a still-woozy-looking Alvarez. "You'll be goin' along too, Alvarez," he said. He pointed out three more, and when he had finished, his five "volunteers" regarded him balefully, but resignedly.

"When we pullin' out?" Alvarez asked.

"Soon."

"You goin' let us carry loaded weapons."

"When the time comes."

For the first time that morning, Alvarez smiled.

3

It was later that same morning that Fargo and his renegade command were about ready to move out.

After seeing to his Ovaro, Fargo had chosen the five best horses he could find for the others, and then, so disgusted had he been at the condition of the stable, he had set a detail to work cleaning it out. Except for his own weapons, those to be issued to the others Fargo had wrapped in a slicker and tied fast to the cantle behind his bedroll. The troopers did not like the idea of riding into hostile territory with their weapons tucked away on Fargo's horse, but they had no choice in the matter.

They were mounted up now on the parade ground, waiting for Fargo to finish his business with Jeb. They had just fashioned a contingency plan in case Fargo had trouble riding out at the head of his renegade command.

"One more thing," Jeb was saying to Fargo. "About that jasper Alvarez. You think you'll be able to handle him once you're out there on the trail along with them other four?"

Fargo glanced shrewdly at Alvarez, studying the man carefully. He sat on his horse well enough, despite his condition. Around his battered head he had wound a dirty bandage. Fargo shrugged.

"You take care of the fort, I'll take care of Alvarez."

"He don't like you none."

"I noticed."

Fargo bid Jeb good-bye, nodded farewell to Angelique and Theresa, then mounted his pinto. Spurring the Ovaro to the head of the small column, he led the troppers out through the gate. Jeb wasted no time closing it behind them.

They were almost across the flat and into the timber when Alvarez spurred his horse alongside Fargo's.

"Fargo," he said, "we want our guns."

"That so?"

"Don't stall. We already decided. None of us is goin' any farther until you give them to us."

Fargo shrugged. "It's your decision."

"You goin' to give us our guns?"

"I'll give them to you when you need them, when we reach Black Feather's camp."

"Okay, men," Alvarez cried to the others, "we're headin' back!"

With wide grins on their faces, the four men yanked their mounts around and pounded back

42

across the flat toward the fort. Fargo pulled up, turned his pinto casually, and sat back to watch. When they had reached to within a hundred or so yards of the fort, Jeb's Hawken cracked and the ground exploded in front of Alvarez's horse.

As Fargo had suggested earlier, Jeb was up on the catwalk with his Hawken, waiting for the troopers to turn back.

Alvarez pulled up his mount. The other riders clattered to a halt alongside him. As they conferred hastily, Jeb sent another round at them. This time one of the troopers lost a hat.

That was cutting it a mite close, Fargo allowed. But he had to laugh when he saw what effect this had on the troopers. Turning their mounts so abruptly they almost collided, they galloped back to rejoin Fargo. Fargo unholstered his Colt, chucked back his wide-brimmed hat, and waited for them to reach him.

Throughout the morning Fargo had been studying the men he had chosen. Now he watched each one even more closely as they approached.

Alvarez was in front. Behind him came a trooper they all called Brick. The reason was obvious: his hair was red, his pale face freckled, his eyes a washed-out blue. He seemed timid most of the time, as startled and wary as a kitten just out of the box.

The trooper behind Brick was Koralski, a husky Pole with a long nose and a battered chin; his eyes glared out at Fargo from under brows so close to his eyes they were barely visible. He seemed perpetually sullen, and the other troopers seemed more than willing to give him a wide berth.

The next trooper was Simonds, a small, round-shouldered man with a slack chin and gray, furtive eyes. He seemed always to be looking over his shoulder, and when he dismounted and moved on afoot, he kept himself bent over, as if he were getting ready to dive for cover or dig himself a hole in the ground. The few words he spoke were more like snarls. The other men seemed to barely tolerate him.

The last rider was Harwood, a tall, lean shiftless no-account with a stringy mustache and chin whiskers yellowed by chewing tobacco. His gaunt face was unshaven, his neck and face grimy. From his accent Fargo knew him as a native of the Ozarks. Of all the five troopers, this one Fargo considered the most dangerous—and possibly the best man with a rifle.

Koralski pushed his mount past Alvarez and pulled it to a shambling stop alongside Fargo. "Guess we should've figured you'd have something like that planned," he said.

"You and the others can stay here if you want."

"That's right. Out here in the middle of nowhere—with no guns to defend ourselves or hunt with. Some choice that is."

"It is still yours to make."

Koralski stared for a long moment at Fargo. Then he took up his reins. "All right, you bastard. Guess you win for now."

In a swipe so sudden Koralski had no chance to duck, Fargo brought up his Colt and caught the big man on the right cheek. The trooper went tumbling backward off his horse and came down on his back, barely conscious. As he stared up through slitted, groggy eyes at Fargo, Fargo cocked his Colt and trained it lazily on him.

"Next time you address me, Koralski, I suggest you keep my pedigree out of it. Do we understand each other?"

Koralski moistened dry lips, then nodded slightly.

Fargo holstered his weapon. "Get on your horse."

As Koralski climbed to his feet and groped somewhat dazedly for his horse's reins, Fargo saw the grim, malicious smile on Alvarez's face. Clearly, he was enjoying Koralski's quick comedown.

"By the way, Koralski," said Fargo. "I want you to ride point."

The man glared wearily at Fargo and nodded.

"We'll be following the river on the other side of that ridge until we're inside Sioux country. Keep your eyes open."

"You ain't gonna give me a rifle?"

"You think I'm crazy?"

"What if I see something?"

"You'll ride back and tell us."

With a last, smoldering glance at Fargo, Koralski rode on ahead and soon disappeared into the timber that clothed the ridge's slope.

A little before sunset they camped along the river. Fargo assigned Brick and Simonds to build the campfire and take care of preparing supper.

After the meal, Fargo opened his bedroll and set it down on pine boughs he gathered together on a slope above the camp. He used his saddle for a pillow and tucked the slicker containing the troopers' weapons under it.

Fargo watched the men below him around the fire. When at last they curled up around it, Fargo strewed pine cones about him and lay down fully dressed, his right hand clasped about the grips of his Colt, his cheek resting on the blade of his bowie.

The attempt to take him came a little after dawn.

It was the sudden urgent chatter of a chipmunk in the branch above Fargo's head that warned him. He opened his eyes in time to see the huge figure of Koralski looming above him, the morning sun glinting on the blade of the Arkansas Toothpick he held high over his head. Fargo started to bring up his Colt, but one well-aimed kick from Karalski sent the Colt flying. As Koralski plunged the blade downward, Fargo rolled out of his slicker and jumped upright, the blade missing by a whisker.

Koralski lunged at him, but Fargo ducked backward and went tumbling down the slope, Koralski racing after him. Fargo scrambled to his feet when he reached the bottom of the slope, and unsheathed his bowie, the remaining troopers swiftly encircling him and Koralski—happy, wolfish grins on their faces. They were expecting Koralski to carve him up slowly, to whittle him down to the bone before finishing him off. And from the easy, graceful way the big Pole stalked Fargo, his double-edged dagger held out lightly before him, it was clear the big trooper was easily capable of doing just that.

Slowly, the two men circled each other, waiting for the chance to make their move. Fargo kept his feet well apart, his right foot slightly advanced, his body and head held well back, knife pointing out and upward, his thumb braced against the bowie's guard. Holding his knife in almost precisely the same way, Koralski suddenly lunged. Fargo parried the thrust, catching the dagger's blade with the back of his bowie, fending the stroke out and away from himself.

Then he thrust himself, but Koralski was as swift as Fargo, and parried just as efficiently. It was no matter. They were simply feeling each other out now. Again they began circling. Fargo could feel the rising sun on the back of his neck, then warming the side of his face as they continued to circle each other. Sweat trickled down the hollow of his back and dripped from his armpits.

There was a sudden, brief flurry, each combatant testing the other's defenses. No damage was inflicted on either, but Fargo came to appreciate the big Pole's lightninglike speed and deftness. No wild cut and stab maniac, he was perfectly willing to wait for his opening, confident he could parry any thrust of Fargo's meanwhile.

Fargo stopped abruptly and slowly lowered his bowie, daring Koralski to make his move. Koralski also halted and straightened. For a moment the two stood there calmly facing each other. Fargo watched Koralski's eyes. The moment they narrowed, though it was only a fraction, he crouched and was just in time to meet Koralski's lightning thrust.

But he was not fast enough.

Koralski's dagger slid in past his guard, and Fargo felt the hot bite of the razor-sharp steel as it sliced through the skin in his left side. He clamped his left elbow down and caught Koralski's wrist between it and his side, then sliced upward with his bowie, probing for the man's gut. But Koralski was already falling back to Fargo's left, dragging Fargo to the ground after him.

The moment Koralski hit, he twisted away from Fargo's grasp and leapt to his feet. Fargo swiped at him; then, crouching, he got to his feet and moved stealthily toward him until the two resumed their circling, Fargo's bowie and Koralski's Toothpick probing the gap between them once again.

Fargo did not glance down at his side. Though he knew he had suffered only a flesh wound, the warm trickle of blood encasing his left side told him that unless he could staunch the flow, he would be gradually enfeebled. In Koralski's eyes Fargo read the first faint glint of triumph. The bloody whittling had begun. A hit anywhere counted, as long as it drew blood. Now if Koralski could move in and slash off Fargo's thumb, slice through the tendons of his right wrist, lay open a piece of his thigh—Fargo would soon be just as dead as if Koralski had managed a thrust to his heart.

Fargo kept moving, hoping. He knew what he had to do ... and soon. He could waste no time going for Koralski's head, neck, or heart. The soft parts of Koralski's body were mainly below the breastbone. A wide, low, sweeping stroke could disembowel Koralski without the danger of Fargo losing his knife if he missed. On the other hand, any slash to the rib cage or above it risked the possibility of Fargo's blade finding bone, which might strip the knife from his hand.

Koralski ducked low, then darted in, his blade flashing. He too was aiming for the soft underbelly. Fargo parried and thrust also, catching the inside flesh of the big Pole's right arm. Koralski pulled back quickly, lightly, his eyes smoking with fury. Fargo saw the blood puddling on the ground before Koralski. Swifter now, he followed Koralski until Koralski was almost running backward.

"You can run, Koralski," Fargo told him, "but you can't hide."

Stung, Koralski held up suddenly, then moved in, thrusting upward. Fargo ducked aside only far enough to protect his vitals and felt the blade's tip catching his belt a second before it sliced into his right side just above the thighbone. Ducking low, Fargo drove in, his bowie sweeping in a long, clean stroke that slit open Koralski's gut. He finished the stroke by slicing up through Koralski's belly button.

Koralski's eyes glazed in horror. He dropped his knife and grabbed at his spilling guts and sat suddenly on the ground. Frantically he tried to gather up his gray, blood-flecked entrails in his two big hands and stuff them back into his belly. Bleeding now from two wounds, Fargo stepped back and watched the doomed man for an instant, then turned away. Knife fights were the bloodiest duels of all, and Fargo had never found their conclusions pleasant.

Even when he won.

Fargo pushed back through the circle of troopers, mildly surprised that not one of them had left during the fight to hustle up the slope to retrieve their weapons. Their confidence in Koralski's skill and their lust for blood had riveted them to the spot.

By noon Fargo had patched up his flesh wounds and he and his renegade command were ready to move out.

But Brick refused to join them. Fargo was astonished at the redhead's sudden obstinacy.

"Get on your mount," Fargo ordered.

"I'm going back to the fort," Brick insisted.

"You know you can't do that. My partner won't let you in."

"I don't care. I ain't going on with you. You're all madmen—killers."

"Maybe so. But what makes you think you can make it back alone? This here timber could be filled with Sioux. They could be all around us."

"I'd prefer the savages to you." He looked distastefully at the other troopers. "To any of you, in fact."

Harwood, already mounted, chuckled meanly.

"Let him go, Fargo. He's gonna piss in his pants if he rides any farther. He's been weepin' and moanin' ever since he showed up at the fort."

"Brick won't be no help to us," agreed Alvarez. "The only reason he deserted was he couldn't stand all the guard duty. Let him go."

"We'll be safer without him," said Simonds, his gray rat-face staring contemptuously at the red-head.

It was clear the young trooper was terrified. Witnessing that knife fight and its result seemed to have been the last straw. What Fargo had hoped when he chose the redhead was that this expedition against the Sioux would bolster his courage. Apparently, it had not been a very good idea.

"All right, Brick. Ride on back if you want."

Eagerly, the trooper snatched at his mount's reins and scrambled up into his saddle. Without a single glance at the other troopers, he spurred back the way they had come. Fargo watched him until he disappeared into the timber, then turned back around in his saddle. The remaining three troopers seemed not at all concerned with Brick's departure.

"Move out," Fargo told them.

"You want me to ride point?" asked Alvarez.

"No," Fargo said. He glanced over at Harwood. The trooper was watching him with cold eyes. "Ride point, Harwood."

The lanky mountaineer kneed his horse ahead of them without comment. The rest followed, Fargo keeping to the rear, one Colt in his belt, the other in his holster.

They had not gone far when the four of them heard a piercing scream that was cut off almost instantly.

It had come from the timber behind them and there was not a man who did not recognize the voice. Brick must have ridden right into a Sioux war party.

"Dismount!" Fargo told the others. "Make for that timber up there!"

No one argued, and in a few minutes Fargo was crouched in the timber, waiting for any sign of the hostiles, the troopers around him glancing hungrily at the rifles wrapped in the slicker on Fargo's pinto.

"They're not comin' this way," Fargo said. "Move out. We'll go after them."

"Give us our guns first."

Fargo considered his options. If he gave the men their rifles and side arms, it was unlikely they would turn their fire on him and reveal their location as well as their presence to the Sioux.

With a shrug, Fargo unwrapped the guns and ammunition and issued them. Then they tied up their mounts and moved back down the slope and into the timber moving in the direction Brick's scream had come from.

They had not gone more than a quarter of a mile when they heard the beat of drums and the wild cries of the Sioux war party ahead of them. Before long, they could smell the smoke of their campfire. Creeping closer, they soon found themselves peering down a small slope at a clearing where the war party was setting up camp.

They were Blackfeet, not Sioux. Fargo could tell from their black moccasins and their war paint.

Beside Fargo, Alvarez turned to the others and muttered, "Blackfeet!" He sounded alarmed—more alarmed than if this were a Sioux war party.

"Yep," said Harwood, wetting his thumb and forefinger and touching the sight of his rifle. "Recognize them bastards anywhere."

There were four Blackfeet in all, decked out in their most colorful war regalia. They were clearly happy in their work as they continued to dance around what was left of Brick. He was hanging from a limb, head down. What had been his head was now a charred side of beef, and the area about his crotch was black with dried blood.

It was ironic. In running from one terror, Brick had stumbled on a far worse horror. Considering their lamentable record, Fargo felt little responsibility for the safety of any of these troopers. They were all expendable as far as he was concerned. But Fargo pitied this pathetic trooper.

Alvarez said, "Any man who runs is always too scared to see where he is going."

Beside him, Simonds shuddered. "That poor bleedin' son of a bitch."

"Split up," Fargo said. "We'll take them from all sides."

"Hell. Leave them," Alvarez said. "They ain't nothin' we can do for Brick now."

"Shut up," said Harwood, his eyes glittering eagerly.

Fargo told Alvarez to circle around and come at

53

the Blackfeet from the other side, with Simonds coming from the east and Harwood from the west. Fargo promised to give them ten minutes to get in place before he opened up on the Blackfeet.

"Just like a turkey shoot," said Harwood, grinning.

The men moved out, and as soon as Fargo judged them to be in place, he lifted his Sharps to his shoulder, sighted carefully on the closest Blackfoot—a big buck with his back to him—and opened fire. The .52-caliber round slammed the brave forward into the fire. A quick flurry of gun fire from all sides cut down the other two, but one Blackfoot, even though he was wounded, managed to keep low after the first rattle of gunfire and dart into the surrounding timber a few yards below Fargo.

There was no time for reloading his Sharps. Leaving the rifle, Fargo unholstered his Colt and slipped swiftly through the timber to cut off the fleeing Blackfoot. As he was cutting across a tiny clearing in the timber, the rustle of a branch being pushed aside alerted him.

He swung to his right, bringing his Colt around as he did so. The Blackfoot hurled himself at Fargo, his skinning knife flashing in his hand. Fargo fired, but his bullet seemed to have no effect on the Indian as he slammed Fargo backward to the ground. The back of Fargo's head struck a rock hidden in the tall grass. Dazed, he watched helplessly as the Blackfoot straddled him. The lower half of the Indian's face was shot away and all Fargo could see were his merciless black eyes as he raised his gleaming knife over his head.

At that moment Alvarez and Simonds materialized out of the timber behind the Blackfoot and swiftly held up to watch the Blackfoot finish off Fargo.

Instead, the Blackfoot whirled to face them.

Fargo felt again the Colt's heavy grips in his palm. In a reflex action so swift he was hardly aware of it, he cocked and fired up at the Blackfoot, catching him under the ribs. The round coursed up through his lungs and exited from his neck in an explosion of blood and sinew.

Before the two troopers could bring up their own weapons, Fargo was on one knee, his Colt, cocked and ready, trained on them. The two men said nothing as they dropped their weapons to the ground. Only then did Fargo become aware of the cold sweat standing out on his forehead.

These two bastards—white men, supposedly—had been willing to stand by and watch that Blackfoot slit his throat.

4

As Fargo stood up, Harwood pushed through the brush to join them. Dangling from his belt were three Blackfoot scalps. When Harwood saw the dead Blackfoot at Fargo's feet, he bent quickly and scalped him as well. Fargo did nothing to stop him, then led the men back to the Blackfoot camp to pick up their medicine bags and claim their war ponies. The Blackfeet were the enemies of every Indian in the region. Fargo had a feeling these trophies would come in handy with the Sioux.

When the troopers returned to their own mounts, Fargo did not make them give up their weapons. He simply took their knives from them and emptied the firing chambers of their rifles and side arms, pocketing the ammunition.

As they set out once again, Harwood pulled alongside Fargo.

"We sure as hell ain't gonna surprise them Sioux with all this horseflesh kickin' up dust."

"Maybe not."

"You want to get us all killed. That it?"

"Frankly, Harwood, I don't give a shit if any of you make it back."

"Well, if it's suicide you're after, mister, why not give me a bullet and I'll end it for you right here? And you can bet on it, I'll be a helluva lot cleaner and quicker than them damn Sioux."

"I don't doubt it, Harwood. But don't go getting your bowels in an uproar. It ain't suicide I'm plannin'."

"Then what in hell're you up to?"

"We got four Blackfeet scalps, still bloody. And we got the medicine bag from each buck. And to top it all off, we got their fine war ponies."

"So?"

"How long you been out here, Harwood?"

"Less'n three months."

"Then I guess you wouldn't figure to know how much the Sioux hate the Blackfeet. Or that we probably saved Black Feather's Sioux some grief when we took out that Blackfoot war party."

"You mean they was meaning to raid the Sioux camp?"

"What else would a Blackfoot war party be doing in Sioux country?"

Harwood shrugged. "I'm listenin'."

"I figure now our best bet is to ride into Black Feather's camp and present him with the Blackfoot ponies and show off the scalps. That should give us a real standing in his eyes."

"Just like that, huh?"

Fargo nodded. "We'll smoke the pipe then and become allies to the Sioux, at least for now—as long as we don't tell them why we've come."

"What about them kids and the settlers?"

"The thing to do is keep our eyes and ears open and make our move when we get a chance."

"Seems like you're playin' this pretty damn close to your vest."

"Why not? Look who my playin' partners are."

Harwood scowled. "I don't like it. This is sure as hell goin' to be ticklish. Ridin' right in among them redskins. Just like they was human beings."

"You'd better act like they were. I know Black Feather from way back. We're on good terms. And he speaks pretty good English."

"An' he hates the bluecoats and settlers."

"Why shouldn't he? What have they ever brought him or his people but disease, rotgut, false promises, and death?"

"You sound like an Injun lover."

"All you have to know, Harwood, is that I trust Black Feather a damn sight more than you—or your two companions. Right now, I suggest you tell the others what I just told you."

As Harwood left Fargo's side and rode on ahead to tell the others, Fargo conceded to himself that the lanky mountaineer was probably right to feel uneasy at Fargo's plan. Once in Black Feather's camp, they would be in the soup. They'd need their wits and a good helping of luck to get them back out again.

*　　*　　*

The Sioux found them before they found the Sioux.

The Blackfoot ponies were strung out between the troopers and Alvarez, who was riding point. It was dusk and they were just quitting a pass, heading down a wide trail that opened into a valley below them, when the Sioux riders materialized out of the timbered slopes above them.

Fargo told the men to halt, chucked his hat back off his forehead, and sat his pinto patiently. At that, the bonneted warrior leading the Sioux rode directly toward him.

The Sioux had already noted the Blackfoot war ponies, and as he pulled up beside Fargo, Fargo displayed the four scalps he had taken from Harwood, then opened up his saddlebag and pulled forth the four Blackfoot medicine bags.

"Tell your chief Skye Fargo has come with gifts for his old friend, Black Feather."

"You Skye Fargo?"

Fargo nodded.

"You bring gifts?"

Fargo nodded and indicated the four ponies. As Fargo had presumed, they made an impressive bunch. One of them, a brown-and-white paint, was almost as handsome as Fargo's Ovaro.

The Sioux nodded and gave instructions to another brave, who wheeled his pony and galloped ahead. Then, with their Sioux escort, Fargo and the three troopers left the pass behind and descended to the valley. Less than a mile farther on, they came to the Sioux village and were led into it past curious squaws, old men, and young children. At last Fargo pulled up in front of Black Feather's lodge.

The chief, arms folded, was standing outside, waiting. He had heard the good news, it seemed, and his eyes gleamed as he regarded the four Blackfoot ponies. Dismounting, Fargo greeted the chief with much ceremony and some warmth. After the amenities and without saying a word about the ponies, Black Feather looked with cold eyes upon the three troopers.

"Why you bring bluecoats?" Black Feather asked. "Is Skye Fargo now scout for army?"

"No, Black Feather. These men are deserters. They run from American flag. No longer do they serve the United States army. I meet them on trail." Fargo smiled. "Later we meet Blackfoot war party." Reaching back to his saddle, Fargo produced the scalps and presented them, along with the Blackfoot medicine bags, to the chief.

The chief took them, then held them up so those crowding around his lodge could see them also. He said something to the braves and squaws that excited them. There was a shout and then a series of spine-tingling yells. Fargo took all this for approval.

Holding the scalps and medicine bags and still having said nothing about the ponies, the chief pushed aside the entrance flap and invited the four of them into his lodge. Leading the troopers, Fargo followed Black Feather inside.

As Fargo had predicted to Harwood, after the chief's two squaws brought them each a bowl of boiled dog meat, Black Feather brought out his ancient, ceremonial pipe, lit it, took a few puffs, them passed it around. This took a while. Then Black Feather put aside the pipe and looked long and hard at Fargo.

"Does Fargo still seek those who kill his mother and father?"

"Yes."

"How many you seek now?"

"Two, Chief."

The barest trace of a smile appeared on the Sioux's craggy visage.

It had been years since Fargo had come upon Black Feather and his tough Sioux band, made his peace with him, and then continued his search for those four men the chieftain had just mentioned. Yet Black Feather looked barely a year older. The only difference in his appearance was a thin, barely visible scar that ran from his left cheekbone to the corner of his mouth. Fargo could imagine the pride with which the chief wore such a sign of his exploits.

"These Blackfeet," the chief said. "They come to raid Sioux. We hear of them. We wait."

"You need wait no longer, Black Feather."

"These Blackfeet are evil warriors. They poison the ground they walk on. Even the birds of the forest fly from them. Their women are whores, fit only for the beds of the coyote. But it is true also— they have many fine horses."

Fargo nodded.

"I see the Blackfoot war ponies you bring. One among them is very fine."

"The paint?"

The chief smiled. "Yes."

"He is yours, Chief."

"And the others?"

"They are gifts for those wariors you favor."

Black Feather beamed and got to his feet. Like a kid coming downstairs on Christmas morning, he could barely restrain himself as he pushed past Fargo and out of the lodge. Fargo and the troopers got up and followed out after him. The chief gathered up the reins of all four of the ponies and inspected them carefully.

More than satisfied, Black Feather began calling out the names of Sioux warriors. As the lucky braves thrust forward eagerly through the crowd that surrounded the ponies, the chief handed each one the reins of the pony he had decided the brave should have. He did so with lordly benevolence, the pleasure he took in dispensing such wealth causing his lined face to glow.

Watching the pleased chieftain, Fargo found himself almost regretting the double-dealing he was planning.

Later, a huge bonfire was lit and the Sioux feasted and danced around it in celebration of the death of their hated enemies and the acquisition of their war ponies and scalps. Then, much later, Black Feather personally escorted Fargo through the darkness to an empty lodge on the perimeter of the village. It was a small one, but Fargo thanked the chief for his hospitality.

As the chief left him, Fargo staked his pinto out in front of the lodge, then hauled his saddle and bedroll into it. Not long before, Fargo had seen the three troopers being shown to a lodge farther down the line. It had not taken long for the chief to recognize Fargo's contempt for the deserters. But now, as Fargo unrolled his sleeping bag, he found himself thinking not of the three troopers, but of the two kids and the settlers.

Throughout the festivities and his long ride through the camp, he had kept his eyes open, but had seen no sign of them. Were they already dead? he wondered. Had Fargo made this dangerous pilgrimage for nothing?

Fargo was still mulling this over when the entrance flap was flung back and a tall, slim Indian girl entered. Startled, then intrigued, Fargo said nothing as she came to a halt before him.

"Black Feather send me to you," she said, her voice so soft it was barely audible.

Fargo smiled. In payment for the ponies, no doubt. He wondered if the troopers were being as well rewarded.

The girl was wearing a deerskin robe and moccasins. She stepped lightly out of the moccasins and let the robe fall to the ground. The only light came from the opening in the top of the lodge, but it was enough for Fargo to get a pretty good look at the naked woman standing before him. Her dark pubic patch seemed to glow like wet coal. Her small breasts were tight, their nipples erect and surrounded by large dark areolas. She was young, almost as tall as he—unusual for an Indian woman—and as slim as a willow sapling. In the dim light, her silken, burnished skin glowed like satin, and he knew at once she was not Sioux, but a Crow.

"What are you called?" he asked.

"Crow Woman."

"I am pleased to meet you, Crow Woman. You please my eyes."

She smiled and her dark eyes glowed. "How do they call you?"

"Skye Fargo. Call me Skye."

She moved closer.

Fargo smelled the sweet scent of the willow bark on her. Many of the tribes used a solution of willow bark, sometimes mixed with borax, to cleanse the skin of blemishes. It was as if her body exuded a faint but palpable perfume: musky, hard to define, but definitely arousing. He looked her up and down as she stood before him, waiting, and let the fire in his loins build.

He swiftly skinned himself, reached up, took her thighs in his hands, and gently folded her down beside him on his bedroll. She was pliant and warm. He kissed her full on the lips, bending her back as he did so. He was pleased to find she was no stranger to a white man's kiss. Her mouth worked sensually as she returned his kiss with a powerful, wanton ardor.

Then she pulled away and lay back on the blanket, gazing up at him out of her large, almond-shaped eyes. They seemed to pull him closer to her until they were large enough to contain all of him. He chuckled and kissed her on each trembling eyelid, then ran his hand over the mounds of her breasts and down across her silken belly to the soft, pulsing warmth below.

She moaned so softly it sounded like the wind sighing through the pine tops. Her flesh came alive to his caresses and she began to undulate under him. He kissed her lips, her cheeks, the tender hollow of her neck. Slipping lower, his tongue darted across her hardened nipples, then moved wetly along her abdomen, feeling its satiny skin ripple beneath his lips. Then, moving still lower, his lips probed and explored as he heard her begin to moan softly. Then came a sharp gasp of pleasure as he moved in deeper and began laving her inner lips. Her trembling hands found his head, and her fingers were soon entangled in his thick black locks as she began heaving under him.

The thighs beneath Fargo's mouth arched and swiveled. He gave them room. Sighing, she spread her legs on either side of his head. Then her hands moved from his hair down along his body to his buttocks, pulling him up onto her. Bending to his face and head, her tongue began teasing him. Planting his knees between her squirming thighs, he felt her ready and moist and heaving upward with desperate anticipation.

Reaching down, she grasped the turgid length of his erection with one hand, using her other to fondle her pubes and spread them for his entry. Then, lifting violently, she flung herself against him just as he lunged forward and down, impaling her, feeling the incredible warmth of her swallowing him completely, sucking him in deeper and deeper. Singing out her delight, Crow Woman wrapped her arms tightly around his back, pulling him down against her breasts, her long body undulating beneath him in wild abandonment. Her nails raked his back for a while; then she reached down to claw at the flesh of his pumping buttocks, thrusting him still deeper into her while her thighs splayed wide on the bedroll beneath her. Snaking his tongue inside her gasping mouth, Fargo increased his wild pace while Crow Woman, equally frenzied, arched her back and pumped up and down, undulating faster—faster—until finally Fargo felt himself lifting inexorably to his own climax.

The hot urgency in his loins exploded in a release so delicious he moaned and cried out softly. Beneath him, as he continued to pulse wildly within her, Crow Woman bucked and cried out in turn, her small white teeth visible in a tight grimace of delight.

A moment later, satiated, they collapsed into each other's arms, the dusky smell of their lovemaking filling the lodge. For a while they stroked and caressed, kissing each other lightly, murmuring contentedly.

At last Fargo dozed.

He came awake fully alert. Crow Woman's head was bent over his thighs. What had awakened him was the electric feel of her tongue as it brushed the tip of his small but building erection.

"What're you doin' there?" he asked, as if he didn't know.

She lifted her head and turned to look at him. "I want to wake you," she said.

"Well, that sure is one helluva nice way to do it, I must admit." Fargo lay back down. "You just go right on. Don't let me distract you."

She laughed. "You are awake, then?"

"Wide awake."

She moved up quickly beside him, her long black hair falling over his head and shoulders like a musky tent. "You must take me away from here," she said.

"That so?"

"Yes. I will be good to you. You see how I am. I can cook, sew. I make your lodge warm and your body too. You will never be sorry."

"You don't like it here with Black Feather?"

"For three years now I am captive woman. The young braves will not take me in marriage. They use me when they cannot get Sioux woman to take them in marriage. They say I am whore—that all Crow women are whores."

"I'll take you with me," Fargo said.

She lifted off him and gazed down at him, eyes wide in sudden joy and relief. "You not lie?"

"I need your help, Crow Woman. In return for that, I will take you with me. Even better, if you help me, I will see to it that you get back to your people."

Her eyes seemed to grow deeper. For a moment it was as if they were devouring him.

"Will you help me?"

She nodded eagerly. "What must I do?"

"Help me find and rescue the two small children Black Feather just captured—and the settlers with them."

He saw the sudden caution and wariness in her eyes, but she did not let it discourage her.

"This I will do," she told him.

"Where are the children? I haven't seen them since I rode in."

"The man child and the little squaw live now in the lodge of Little Bird and his wife. For many moons they want son to take care of them when Little Bird can no longer kill the buffalo and deer. This young brave will make fine warrior and a mighty hunter. And the little squaw someday bring Little Bird much wealth when it comes time for her to marry."

"How far is Little Bird's lodge?"

"On other side of village."

"What about the settler and his wife?"

"The settler is dead and his woman sits in Fox Woman's lodge. She looks but does not see. She listens but does not hear. The spirit is gone from her body. She cannot use the flint to build a fire. She is good only for gathering wood."

Fargo could imagine what horror the settler's wife must have endured. But at least now she was out of it. Her mind had snapped and, locked away so securely within herself, all the horror that went on around her from now on would be unknown to her. The Indians, both fearing and respecting one so afflicted, would keep her fed and clothed and treat her with surprising consideration.

"There was another man, an old one," Fargo said.

Crow Woman brightened slightly. "Yes. He is alive. He is strong. Like old tree. He not bend or cry out. The Sioux will not kill him I think. They feed him and some come to look at him. His soul is good."

Fargo nodded. Indians tortured their prisoners to see what they were made of, how strong their medicine was. A captive who wept and pleaded for his life gained only their contempt. Indeed, killing anyone so craven gained them no honor. It was no more significant than cracking a louse.

Fargo had known of one mountain man who had prevented his death by the simple expedient of howling out his defiance at the top of his powerful lungs as the astonished chief stood before him. So startled and impressed had the chief been by this bravado, he decided against killing a man with such strong medicine.

"Tomorrow," Fargo told her, "you must help free the two boys and the old man."

"You say tomorrow?"

"Yes."

"You must not wait so long, Skye."

"Why not?"

"You must go now, before Black Feather kill you."

Fargo sat up. "I am his guest. I kill his enemy the Blackfoot, and I bring him many fine ponies to give to his young warriors. Why does the chief want to kill me?"

"Owl Woman was the daughter of Black

Feather. She was taken by bluecoat when she swim in river. She try to escape. But he catch her. Then he rape her and kill her. This happen two moons ago. Her sister see this bluecoat when he ride in with you. She tell chief after he take you to this lodge. Chief send me to you so you will stay in village with other bluecoats."

"If he's so anxious to kill us, why is he waitin'? Why don't he kill us right now? Tonight?"

"Running Deer was Owl Woman's man. Now he is gone from village with hunting party. Soon he will come back. Then he will be one to kill bluecoat who kill his woman."

"Which trooper did it?"

"The little one. He is small and his shoulders are bent. He has gray face and move like mole."

Simonds.

"Already Black Feather send for Running Deer," Crow Woman continued. "When he comes back, all of you must die."

"Why all of us?"

"Black Feather do not want other Indians to know Black Feather dishonors his hospitality."

Fargo understood at once. No chief would have it get out that a guest of his met death while under the protection of his hospitality. But since no Indian of Black Feather's band would reveal such a lapse, it would not matter if Black Feather killed the three troopers, since word of it would never get out to stain his reputation. But if Fargo were to escape, the shame of what Black Feather had done would get out.

Which meant Fargo too must die.

5

Fargo lay back down. He needed to get some thinking done. He was in a nest of tarantulas, and he figured he'd better get the hell out before the chief tarantula finished him off.

Desire stabbed his loins like a hot poker. He lifted his head and saw Crow Woman brush her hair back and smile up at him, her dark eyes regarding him fondly.

"Lay back, Skye. I finish now what I start. To thank you for taking me back to my people."

"I ain't done that yet."

"You will. You are very brave man. You have powerful medicine. Lay still now."

She ducked her head. Fargo lay back and found himself opening his legs still wider as Crow Woman's lips began once again to lick voraciously on his rapidly growing shaft, plunging her mouth down over his erection, engulfing it with a soft,

71

clinging pressure as she grabbed hold of his thighs.

Fargo gave up trying to hold back then as he felt his hips writhing, stirring, swaying—his whole lower body aching in a sweet agony of expectation. Soon, Crow Woman's seemingly disembodied lips, her mouth, her throat were devouring him completely, drawing his vital juices down to his groin while she continued to cling fiercely to his wildly gyrating buttocks.

And then he gave one final, massive, upward thrust as Crow Woman continued to devour him . . .

"The old man's name is Matthew," Fargo told Crow Woman.

He was sitting up now and Crow Woman was resting back against his shoulder and chest, his arm draped over her silken breast, one finger idly flicking her nipple.

"His daughter back at the fort said he could ride pretty well for a gent his age. So we'll need a horse for both of you. The two children can ride with me and the old man."

"I will see to the old one," Crow Woman told him. "And the horses. Crow Woman has for long time plan this. When she see you and bluecoats ride in, she think maybe now is time." She turned her head to look more closely at Fargo with her unfathomable eyes. "And when Black Feather send Crow Woman to you, she know she is right."

"Where will you be waiting with the horses?"

"On the other side of the river. In the willows.

The old man will be with me. And the young brave and his sister, too."

"How you goin' to manage that?"

"The two young ones know me. They will come with me."

"What about Little Bird and his squaw? Won't they raise hell?"

"They will not know. I will not waken them when I take young brave and little squaw."

"But suppose you do wake them?"

"Fargo not to worry. Crow Woman know what to do."

A menacing edge had crept into her voice. He looked sharply at her. "You got an account to settle with Little Bird?"

"Little Bird and his squaw buy me from brave who capture me," Crow Woman replied, her obsidian eyes smoldering. "For them I gather wood and carry water. Soon I cook for them and clean their lodge and scrape their skins. Many things I do—from before sun come up until it go down. But still I must work more. Little Bird wait until his squaw sleep, then he tell me I must sleep with him. When his squaw find out, she beat me many times and drive me from lodge. She say I am devil. She say all Crow Squaws are whores. This happen in winter. For many weeks I sleep under the stars. For blanket I have only snow."

Fargo nodded. He now understood perfectly. Crow Woman would be able to take care of Little Bird and his squaw if it came to that.

He bent and kissed Crow Woman on the lips. They opened and held his lips, drawing him into her. Her arms snaked up and closed about his neck. Before he knew it, Fargo was moving onto her and she was opening her thighs for him once again and he was entering her with such ease it felt like he was coming home after a long journey.

That was how good it felt. . . .

Smiling, Crow Woman got up, stepped into her slippers, and wrapped her robe around her. Without a word she slipped out of the lodge. Fargo got to his feet and went to the entrance and peered out. Crow Woman was gone—as if she had vanished into thin air.

Dressing swiftly, Fargo left the tepee and made his way along the perimeter of the village to the troopers' lodge. Pushing into it, he was just able to make out three shapes huddled in the darkness, asleep. He started across the lodge toward them but did not get far. A forearm dropped over his head and closed about his neck. Gasping, Fargo staggered back and twisted wildly as the three men pulled him to the ground.

Still grappling furiously, Fargo found himself looking up at Simonds' gray face. Simonds had both hands tightening about his neck and Harwood was kneeling on his chest. Standing upright beyond them was Alvarez, his white teeth visible as he smiled.

Fargo waited patiently for Simonds to release him, aware that if he struggled it would only encourage Simonds to increase the pressure on his windpipe. He felt the blood pounding in his temple, and the faces of the three men began to swim sickeningly about him in the dark lodge.

Simonds released him, then stood up, the Trailsman's Colt in his right hand, its muzzle aimed down at Fargo's head. Harwood took his knee off Fargo's chest and stepped back also. Fargo gasped for breath, then tried to swallow. It was not easy. It felt as if a razor was still lodged in his throat.

"Go ahead, Simonds," Fargo rasped painfully. "Pull that trigger and bring the Sioux running. There's some out there been waiting to get their hands on you, from what I heard."

Frowning, Simonds took a step back, glancing furtively at Alvarez as he did so.

"Maybe so," Alvarez replied, taking the gun from Simonds' hand. "But we've got the edge now, *Mister* Fargo."

Fargo pushed himself to a sitting position and rubbed his throat gingerly. "That's all you've got. An edge."

"We're gettin' out of here," said Harwood. "As soon as we get back our ammunition."

"Where is it?" asked Alvarez.

"In my saddlebags, back in my lodge."

Alvarez glanced at Simonds and gave him a short nod. Simonds moistened his lips, nervously brushed his thinning hair back, then slipped out of the lodge. Fargo tried to get himself comfortable. His throat was still pretty sore and it felt as if Harwood might have cracked one of his ribs.

Fargo was furious with himself for having walked so blindly into this trap. He blamed that wild session he had just had with Crow Woman. It had damn well softened his brain—along with that other part of his anatomy.

The smile on Alvarez's face broadened. "We was just comin' for you. Nice you could save us the trip."

Harwood stepped closer. "You said something back there to Simonds. Something about these Indians here looking for him. What was that all about?"

Fargo told them what Crow Woman had told him—that Simonds had been recognized by one of Black Feather's daughters as the trooper who had raped and killed her sister some months before.

"And you was comin' over here to warn him?"

"I didn't say that."

"No, you didn't. Fact is, you was probably gettin' ready to deliver him to your redskin friends."

Fargo did not bother to reply.

Panting from fear as well as exertion, Simonds burst back into the lodge, carrying Fargo's saddlebags. He wasted no time emptying out the boxes of cartridges and distributing them to his companions.

As soon as the three troopers had loaded their weapons, they stepped back and looked with triumphant eyes down at Fargo.

"We sure been waitin' for this," said Simonds, moving closer. He still held Fargo's revolver in his hand.

"Just don't pull that trigger," Harwood warned him.

"Don't worry."

Simonds took another step closer and raised the gun over his head. Fargo coiled his muscles under him and waited for Simonds to take just one more step. At the same time he reached back with his right hand and rested it on the handle of his bowie.

In the dark lodge, the three troopers had not seen, and so had not taken from him, the knife still resting in its scabbard on his belt—and when he reached back, they saw in that movement only a feeble attempt to brace himself for the coming blow.

"Hurry up, Simonds," Harwood said. "Do it and be done with it."

This was enough to goad Simonds. Raising the revolver still higher, he took another step forward.

Fargo drew his knife and jumped up. The gun was already descending. Warding off the blow with his upraised left forearm, Fargo buried the bowie into Simonds' stomach. The man dropped the gun and tried to scream as Fargo flung him backward off the knife, but all he could manage was a soft, terrified whimper as he struck the ground. Fargo dived for his revolver, and when he brought it up, he found the two troopers had vanished.

A moment later Fargo heard them heading toward the river, pulling their horses after them. Dogs nearby began barking. In a moment an answering chorus of howling and barking canines erupted, the alarm spreading rapidly from lodge to lodge. Harwood and Alvarez were not doing a very good job of sneaking out of the Sioux village.

"You must be Fargo," the old man said to him as Fargo, leading his pinto, splashed through the shallows and stepped up into the willows.

"And you'd be Matthew Wayland," Fargo replied, shaking the old man's hand and nodding at the two wide-eyed children. "You'll be happy to know that your daughter is safe at the fort and counting on your return."

"Much obliged, Mister Fargo." Then the old man looked past Fargo at the Sioux village across the river. "What's all that commotion over there?"

"The troopers I rode in with have run into a little trouble."

"Those poor men!"

"Yeah," Fargo said, thinking their bad luck was his good fortune. "If we hurry, while the Sioux are busy punishing them, we can get a good start."

The old man frowned. "I suppose you're right."

"I know I am. And don't worry about those men. There's an explanation, but it'll have to wait."

Crow Woman had managed to steal the ponies they needed and was standing close by with the two children. The ponies were already saddled, Indian fashion: a heavy mat covered by a single blanket.

"Can you ride on this here Indian saddle?" Fargo asked the old man.

"Well enough."

Fargo turned to the little girl and boy. Fargo knew the girl to be Beth, the boy Sam. Sam was eight, Beth six.

"Who wants to ride with Mister Wayland?" Fargo asked them.

"I will," Sam said. His face looked pinched and frightened, but his eyes betrayed excitement as well.

Wayland mounted up and Fargo lifted the boy up onto the saddle in front of him. Then Fargo turned to the girl. He thought for a moment she was going to cry. Her large brown eyes were as big as horse chestnuts.

"Where is my mother?" she asked, her words perfectly articulated.

"She's not coming."

A large tear moved down her cheek.

Fargo went down on one knee beside her. "Are you strong enough to hang on to my neck?"

She hesitated only a moment, then nodded.

"Okay. Grab hold."

As soon as the tiny arms were about his neck, Fargo swung up onto the pinto, then gently lifted Beth around and planted her down firmly on the saddle before him.

"Hold on to the saddle horn if you want," he told her.

"Thank you," she said.

"Call me Skye."

She nodded dutifully.

Crow Woman had already mounted.

Fargo glanced over to her. The two exchanged nods and moved out.

As they left the willows, Fargo glanced back. Another large bonfire had been started in the middle of the village, and above the steady drumbeat Fargo thought he heard a man screaming.

He could not be sure, of course. And he hoped he was wrong. Still, even if that had been Alvarez or Harwood, it would make no difference. The important thing now was for Fargo to take advantage of the Sioux's diversion and get these children and Matthew Wayland back to the fort—and if that meant riding his pinto and these other two ponies into the ground, so be it.

They reached the fort at dusk the following day. Though all three mounts were lathered pretty thoroughly and a bit unsteady, they were still on their feet when Jeb opened the fort's gates to them. They rode into the fort.

Just in time.

As the gate swung shut, a distant rifle shot hammered a slug into its side. Then came a flurry of rifle fire. From the catwalk high on the fort's walls, two troopers called down to Jeb. Black Feather had just broken from the timber and was galloping across the flat in full cry.

Hurriedly, Fargo sent Matthew Wayland, the two children, and Crow Woman on a run toward the wagons. Before they reached them, Theresa and Angelique burst from the wagons and hurried to meet them.

"You've moved the wagons," Fargo noted, turning back to Jeb.

"I know."

Grabbing his Sharps, Fargo started up the ladder to take a look-see for himself. Jeb quickly grabbed his arm and hauled him back down.

"Hold on, Fargo! Don't go up there!"

"Why the hell not?"

"It's too dangerous."

"The Sioux ain't that good shots."

"It isn't the Sioux I'm talkin' about."

"What do you mean?"

Jeb pointed to the barracks on the other side of the parade ground. "I got six troopers holed up in the barracks. They're all armed. They been takin' potshots at us whenever they get the chance."

Fargo glanced toward the barracks. It looked harmless enough until, looking more closely, Fargo saw the shattered windows. Looking back at the wagons, he realized why Jeb had relocated them. The sutler's store now stood between them and the barracks.

"How'd they get the guns?"

"Blaine and those who sided with him attacked the wagon while I was hauling provisions from the sutler's store."

"Did Blaine hurt anyone?"

"He would've, but that Angelique beat him and the others off. Fact is, I think she winged one of them. She's a tigress, that one."

"How many troopers are sticking with you?"

"Four."

"You trust them?"

"As far as I could throw a mule team. But they probably figure stickin' with me and you is their best chance of gettin' out of this with a full head of hair."

Fargo and Jeb moved up to a peephole beside the gate. Looking through it, Fargo saw that Black Feather and his warriors had pulled up about three hundred yards from the fort. It was a typical move. What they were doing now was pumping up their courage, letting out yells and brandishing their coup sticks. A few of the more excitable young braves were occasionally charging closer, firing as they came. But the fort's return fire turned them back easily enough.

Fargo glanced up at the troopers on the catwalk. "How many of them troopers did you say we can count on?"

"Four."

"With you and me, that won't be much." Fargo frowned suddenly.

Black Feather was gathering his warriors around him, haranguing them excitedly. It was clear he was pumping fire into their guts for a frontal assault on the fort. The chief stopped talking, swung his pony around, and spurred to the head of his braves.

"Here he comes," said Jeb, "the crazy son of a bitch."

Fargo turned and bolted for the ladder. He wasn't going to worry about the marksmanship of those deserters holed up in the barracks behind them. Right now they had other problems. He heard Jeb clambering up behind him, cursing at the risk they were taking. By the time they reached the catwalk, Black Feather and his forces were less than a hundred yards from the fort.

"Aim for their horses," Fargo yelled to the troopers. "Unhorse the bastards!"

Fargo then rested his sights on the nearest pony and squeezed off a shot. The horse went down, its rider somersaulting over its head. Fargo heard a dim cheer erupting around him, followed by a rattle of fire that brought down three more ponies and their riders.

The charge broke.

Fargo sighted on Black Feather, fired, but saw no result as the chief and the rest of the Sioux wheeled and beat a retreat back across the flat. As Fargo watched Black Feather galloping off, he could not help noticing that the chief was riding one of the Blackfoot war ponies Fargo had presented to him.

"Hold your fire!" Fargo called to the others.

The firing tailed off, and he looked around him at the four troopers. They didn't look like much, but they were all Fargo and Jeb had. It would not be easy holding off Black Feather's band if the chief made another attempt to storm the fort under cover of darkness. And Fargo was pretty sure that was just what the wily old chief had in mind.

Unless Fargo could work out some kind of deal with him, that is.

6

As they were climbing back down the ladder, Fargo saw the troopers who had been holed up in the barracks making a break for the sutler's store. They vanished behind it and a moment later Fargo and Jeb could hear the shattering of glass and the scraping of chairs from inside as the looting began.

"I'm not worried about the provisions," Jeb said as he reached the ground. "We've already loaded them into the wagons. But they're goin' to get awful sick on that rum in there."

"I hope we can count on that."

"You got something up your sleeve, have you?"

Fargo started for the gate. "Get the wagons ready to move out."

"Where the hell you off to?"

"I'm goin to pay that damn-fool chief a visit."

"You're crazy."

"Maybe. While I'm gone, keep those troopers holed up in the sutler's store. And get the women and the kids ready for a long haul. We'll need water and plenty of provisions, don't forget."

"You wouldn't want to tell me what you're up to, would you?"

"It'd take too long," Fargo said, pulling open the gate and slipping out into the gathering darkness.

Keeping low, the Trailsman kept close to the fort's wall until he reached the timber, them moved parallel with the flat, listening for the sound of Black Feather's camp. It was pitch dark before he heard the mutter of the drums as the Sioux worked themselves into a lather. Not long after, he caught the glow of their campfire ahead of him in the trees.

His bowie in one hand, his cocked revolver in the other, Fargo snaked his way through the brush until he was within thirty yards of the encampment. He did not see Black Feather at first, then caught sight of him sitting apart on the other side of the fire, talking with two of his younger chiefs. They were painted up in their war colors, and the steady beat and the constant chanting as the younger braves circled the fire was beginning to get Fargo's blood up also.

Slowly, steadily, Fargo worked himself around the perimeter of the camp until he was behind the chief. Then he waited until the two chiefs with him moved off. When they did, Fargo crept steadily closer to Black Feather, halting only when he was close enough to be able to reach out and slit the chief's throat.

But he kept his knife sheathed and dug the barrel of his revolver into the old chief's back instead. "The gun's cocked, Black Feather. Don't make any sudden moves."

The startled chief tensed for a moment, then relaxed. "It is Fargo?" he grunted.

"Give that man a ceegar."

"Pull the trigger. My braves will see that you die—but not quick."

"Hell, Chief, I just want to talk. The drums are makin' enough noise to drown out anything we have to say."

"Talk, then."

"You lost some braves today—and some horseflesh. I figure it's time we deal."

"Maybe yes. Maybe no. I listen."

"You got no cause to come after us the way you're doin'."

"I welcome you to my camp. I present you with fine Crow Woman. You thank me by taking Crow Woman and killing Little Bird and his woman when you take young captives. I do not care about the old one. You can have him. He is too brave to kill, but too old to hunt."

"Hold it right there. What was that you said about Little Bird and his woman?"

"You killed them."

Fargo was suddenly annoyed. Crow Woman had said nothing to him about that when he arrived at the willows. She should have told him that she had killed Little Bird and his squaw.

"All right," Fargo sighed. "But I left you someone in exchange—that trooper who killed your daughter. His name was Simonds."

"It was you kill him?"

"Yes."

"That is much. But it is not enough. I must kill all the bluecoats. Running Deer and my other chiefs demand it. And I want Crow Woman back."

Fargo sighed. "I told you. I'm willin' to deal. I'll give you a chance to take many scalps and count many coup tomorrow."

"Speak more."

"Tomorrow I'll pull out of the fort with my friends—and I'll leave the bluecoats to you."

"You give me nothing I do not already have."

"The fort's gate'll be gone. It won't be an obstacle to your brave warriors."

"But are not these bluecoats your white brothers?"

"I told you. They don't follow the flag I follow. They've deserted the army. They're men out of control—good for nothing but rape and pillage."

"This is true. Many times have those bluecoats made the squaws to wail in my village. They rape many, even the young girls. Once they shoot at Little Coyote when he swim in river. He is small brave. He only ride horse for one year. But they kill him. My people see you ride in with them. They think you are one of them."

"The death of Simonds must tell you that I'm not."

Black Feather hesitated a moment, then nodded. "Yes, that is true. Skye Fargo travel alone, not with bluecoats. I will speak to the other chiefs."

"I'll need time to get back to the fort and get the wagons ready."

"Crow Woman. She is with you still?"

"Yes."

"Many times she warm my bed. She is good to a man, even if that man has seen many winters. She has many skills. I think Black Feather want her back."

"No. She's going back to her own people. And I'll take her back. Crow Woman says Black Feather, the Chief of the Creek Sioux, is a great leader of his people. And she says if Black Feather will let her return to her people, it'll bring even more honor upon him. Someday the chief of the Sioux and the Crow will form an alliance to stop the Blackfeet."

"Sioux will never ride to battle with Crow. But the words of Crow Woman are wise. Maybe it is good thing to let Crow Woman go. But I do not think so. Still, I will think on it."

"Then the chief agrees to my bargain?"

"I must speak to Running Deer."

"That ain't much comfort, Chief."

Black Feather straightened his back proudly. "I am the chief of the Creek Sioux. Running Deer will listen to my council."

Fargo realized this was all the assurance he was going to get from the wily old chief. It would have to be enough.

"All right, Chief," Fargo whispered, "it's a deal. I'll be pullin' out now. I suggest you stay sittin' right where you are for a while. If you try to set off an alarm, it could go bad with you."

"I know of the warrior Skye Fargo's skill with knife and gun. Go now. You make deal this time."

Fargo pushed himself back and away from the encampment. The chief was still sitting where he had left him when Fargo finally jumped to his feet and raced off through the timber, back toward the fort.

Fargo flattened himself against the wall of the headquarters building and waited for Jeb to move on past him to the outhouse behind the store—as planned.

Fargo had filled Jeb in by this time, relating all that had transpired since he set out with the five troopers to find the Sioux camp. Jeb's reaction when Fargo had told him of the deal he had made with Black Feather surprised him, however. Jeb had grinned and slapped Fargo on the back, then reminded Fargo those troopers were all deserters, malingerers, and murderers more than likely, who had treated the Sioux Indians around the fort miserably for years.

And now Fargo and Jeb were going to see to it that every one of those poor dumb bastards would die with their boots on in the finest tradition of the U.S. cavalry.

Jeb waved to Fargo. He was in position, less than twenty yards farther on. Fargo motioned to Tyler, one of the few troopers Fargo was sure he could trust. Lugging an oil lamp and an oil can,

Tyler took his prearranged spot behind the sutler's store alongside the outhouse.

From the sound of it, the celebration inside the sutler's store was going full blast. All Fargo wanted now was to arouse the men sufficiently from their revels so they wouldn't be taken by surprise when Black Feather swept into the fort. And also Fargo wanted to give any in there who wanted it the opportunity to join him and the other four troopers.

"Okay, Tyler," Fargo cried.

The trooper poured the coal oil along the backside of the store. Then he stepped back, lit the lamp, and threw it against the oil-slick wall. As the side of the building exploded into flame, he held his arm up to protect his eyes from the fire's blast.

Fargo fired his revolver into the air twice. The combination of the fiery explosion and the two thunderous shots stilled the commotion inside the store. Then came a cry of fire from within, a second later the troopers broke out through the two end windows, tumbling drunkenly over one another as they hit the ground and scrambled to their feet.

"Hold it right there," Fargo shouted.

But only two mem were sober enough to do as Fargo told them. The rest bolted, heading for the stables, Blaine in the lead. When Jeb fired over their heads to slow them down, they returned his fire. In a moment they had vanished into the night. Fargo was not sure, but he thought he saw one or two clinging to bottles as well as firearms as they ran.

"You two," Fargo said, "we're getting out of here. You want to come with us?"

"Where you goin'?" the taller of the two said.

"Fort Laramie."

"You goin' to be in charge."

"Looks like it."

"Then the hell with it," said the other one. "We'll take our chances here."

"They don't look so good."

"What're you drivin' at?"

"Black Feather's out there now, planning to take this fort. He don't like the way some of you men treated his people when this post was active."

"Well, now ain't that just too bad?"

"They're coming in here after you."

"Let 'em come!"

"You're fools."

"Not so foolish we'd put our head back into a noose—and that's what we'd be doin' if we went back to Fort Laramie with you."

"All right, then. Move off. And you better warn the others."

The two men turned and raced toward the barn.

Fargo watched them go for an instant, then waved to Tyler and Jeb. They had no more time to waste.

As Fargo looked back, he saw the blazing gate crumbling, while above it black, billowing clouds of smoke rose into the night sky, filling it with blazing cinders. He had kept his part of the bargain with Black Feather, and it was time to see if Black Feather would keep his.

Fargo turned his pinto into the timber and followed after the wagons. By now they should have been at least a mile ahead of him. He had not ridden far when he heard the deep thunder of Indian ponies as Black Feather and his Sioux charged across the flat. As they swept into the fort, they filled the night with their war cries. Then came the crack of rifle fire.

Fargo urged his Ovaro deeper into the timber, relaxing only when he could hear the rattle of gunfire no longer.

He overtook the wagons an hour later and insisted they keep going. They traveled through that night and all the next day, stopping only long enough to water and grain the horses. When at last Fargo consented to a camp, it was in among a crowd of boulders with a sheer wall at their back—in short, an easily defended high ground.

By the time they were bedded down for the night, the moon was high. Fargo, his saddle on his shoulder and his bedroll under his arm, was heading for a spot he had picked out on a ledge overlooking the camp. That was when Crow Woman approached him.

"You will sleep alone?" She looked up at the moonlit sky. "It will be a cold night."

"Thanks, Crow Woman. I appreciate the thought, but I'm pretty damn tired."

Crow Woman's large, liquid eyes narrowed in suspicion. "You do not like Crow Woman now?"

Fargo put down his saddle and his bedroll. "That ain't it, Crow Woman."

"After we leave fort, your eyes not meet my eyes."

Fargo sighed. "Crow Woman, why in blazes didn't you tell me you killed Little Bird and his squaw?"

She seemed relieved to find it was only this that was bothering him. Clearly she had feared it might be something much more serious. "Why must I tell you?" she said, shrugging. "What does it matter? When I enter the lodge of Little Bird, he wake up. So I kill him and his squaw with knife. I am very quiet. I do not disturb the little ones."

Her eyes gleamed as she spoke, like those of a cat glancing up from a fresh kill. Fargo realized then that Crow Woman had seen in Fargo's coming not only a chance to escape Black Feather, but also to avenge her treatment at the hands of Little Bird and his squaw.

"I wish you'd told me."

Crow Woman turned away. "Then sleep alone, Fargo."

He watched her go, smiling to himself. She was a wild one. And unpredictable. For a moment he almost changed his mind and called her back—until he realized that he really *was* too tired.

Wearily, he picked up his saddle and bedroll and moved up into the rocks.

A little before dawn, he awoke suddenly to hear someone climbing stealthily up the slope to his position. He closed his hand quickly about the grips of his Colt and thumb-cocked it. Jeb and he had worked out a watch for the night, the four troopers each taking a two-hour turn. This did not sound like one of the troopers. The movements were more stealthy. And lighter. It was an Indian, perhaps.

He closed his eyes and pretended to be asleep. The light footfalls ceased. He could feel whoever it was rising to his full height after gaining the ledge. A moment later he was looming over him.

Fargo opened his eyes and in a sudden, lightning-quick thrust jammed his Colt's muzzle violently upward.

"Oh!" Angelique cried, jumping back, her hand going to her stomach where Fargo's Colt had poked her.

Throwing off his blanket, Fargo stood up before her, stark-naked, eyes blazing. Quickly Angelique stepped back, her eyes widening in surprise at his bold and powerful body.

"What in hell're you up to, Angelique?" Fargo demanded. "You're lucky I didn't blow you all the way to hell and back."

"I . . . I couldn't sleep," she stammered.

"Well, I was sleeping real good until I heard you coming."

"But how could you? I was so quiet."

Fargo lowered his gun and, in spite of himself, smiled. "Angelique, you were about as quiet as a Mexican revolution."

"You must sleep very lightly."

"It's an old habit."

"Of course. I should have realized."

He turned back to his bedroll and slumped down, placing his revolver back in its holster. Then he took up his blanket and covered himself. Angelique moved closer and looked down at him.

"Could I . . . join you?"

"You already have. Sit down."

She sat down beside him and rearranged her loose, wide-flaring skirt to make herself more comfortable. She was wearing a white blouse she had left open at the neck, and her dark, lustrous hair was still combed out, as it must have been when she had retired for the night earlier. Fargo could not be absolutely positive, but he had an idea she was not wearing a corset. Despite this, the swell of her breasts under her blouse was more than ample.

"I saw you refuse the Indian woman." Angelique smiled. "I think perhaps she is angry with you."

"She'll get over it."

"I suppose. Theresa is angry also."

"Why in hell would she be angry?"

"Because you left those troopers behind for the Indians to kill."

"I figure the troopers took their share of Indians with them. I warned them Black Feather was out there."

"Did you warn them you were going to burn the gate down to make it easier for the Sioux?"

"No."

"How do you feel about that?"

"I did what I had to do. We're out of that particular rattrap now—and a helluva lot closer to Fort

95

Laramie." There was an edge to his voice when he finished.

"Don't be angry with me, Fargo," Angelique said, her voice soft. "Those troopers were no better than animals. I am glad they are dead and that the Indians killed them. I am also glad we are free of that horrible fort."

He leaned back and looked her over. He was wide awake now. Every part of him. "Anything else you're glad about?"

"Yes."

"And what might that be?"

"That you are so . . . well-endowed and that you don't have any clothes on under that blanket."

"After what you been through, I thought you might have had enough of men."

"Enough of men? No, Fargo. Men are in short supply out here. I sure as hell didn't count Captain Blaine or any of his lice-ridden troopers as men."

"Guess I can understand that."

"Can you?" She rolled deftly over, lifted his blanket, and snuggled closer, then folded the blanket back over her. A second later he felt her hand on his erection and gasped, delighted.

"While I take care of this," she told him, "why don't you help me get out of these clothes? But we don't have to be in too much of a hurry. We have at least an hour yet before dawn."

She flung her head back and lifted her face to his. He kissed her then full on the lips and began unbuttoning her blouse. As he had guessed, she had made things easy for him by not wearing a corset. In a moment, his lips still fastened to hers, he had her blouse off. Their lips still together, he reached down and unbuttoned the side of her skirt. In a moment, her skirt gone, she was peeling off her petticoat. Again, she had made things easy for him. She was wearing no panties and his hand easily found the moist warmth of her muff.

She flung her arms about his neck then, her tongue thrusting deep into his mouth, alive and wanton. Fargo brought his hands up to cup her breasts. They were large and full, like ripe melons. And they seemed to tighten and thrust forward hungrily as his rough fingertips caressed the nipples. She groaned again, sounding deeper now, like a great cat purring, her arms still about his neck, her tongue probing with a reckless urgency that inflamed him. He could smell her. It was the aroma of a woman aroused, and its incense filled his nostrils, arousing him to an even keener pitch.

He broke the kiss and took one of her nipples in his mouth. It grew as hard as a bullet as his tongue flicked at it. Angelique leaned back and opened her legs hungrily, arching up her pelvis against his throbbing erection.

Reaching down, his fingers found the moist, swollen warmth of her pliant labia. Then he reached behind her and thrust her buttocks up as he drove his railroad spike deep into her, impaling her so violently that a sharp, delighted gasp broke from her. At the same time her vaginal muscles grabbed his shaft with the force of a grasping hand. Angelique flung her head back, flung up her legs, and locked her ankles around the small of his back as he knelt over her.

"Deeper, Fargo," she cried, rocking back to take him all the way in. "Deeper!"

Fargo obliged. Then he pulled out. She gasped in dismay and anger. A thin smile on his face, he reentered her, plunging in this time with a fury matching her desire.

"Ah, yes," she told him, urging him on. "That's it, Fargo!"

Again and again he performed the operation, each time just barely clearing her labia before driving his erection home. It felt like it had a mind of its own by this time, plunging in, then withdrawing, only to charge back in once again.

He kept this up as long as he could, then found himself rushing to his orgasm. Angelique flung her head from side to side while he pounded blindly on, rising to his own climax. Abruptly, she became rigid under him. Her inner muscles squeezed his erection so tightly he felt he was not going to be able to withdraw it. He plunged down, hard—harder than before.

With a deep yelp, Angelique climaxed, and a second later Fargo himself was swept over the edge. He became aware of his own pulsing, spasmodic thrusting as he emptied himself into her. It lasted for a long, wondrous moment.

She opened her eyes and looked up at him. In the darkness, he could barely see her eyes. What he saw was more a glow than anything else.

"I can still feel you inside me," she whispered, panting slightly, the tip of her tongue showing through her lips. "I have heard some women say it is not important how big a man is. But don't believe it, Fargo."

"If you say so."

She kept him inside her as she rolled them both over. With a skill and expertise that mildly astonished Fargo, she hauled both legs up and sat back on his erection, gasping with pleasure as she felt him going in still deeper. Soon he had probed so far into her that he wondered if he would ever be able to get out.

Smiling down at him, Angelique began to rotate her hips very slowly. "I'll go slow at first," she told him. "Isn't that nice?"

"I ain't complaining."

"Me neither," she sighed.

Fargo lay back and let Angelique play it her way. She clearly knew what she was doing and was sure as hell enjoying herself, pausing every now and then to hold his erection tightly deep within her to delay his as well as her own climax.

Slowly, steadily, she increased the tempo until at last, her perspiring face gleaming in the darkness, she gave in to her own mounting pleasure and flung herself forward, her long dark hair streaming down over Fargo's head and shoulders, until, with a deep, guttural groan of pleasure, she climaxed, pouring her juices down his shaft and out over his inner thighs in a hot, delicious explosion that sent her falling forward, limp and trembling, onto his chest.

Fargo felt used, but he didn't mind. Now it was his turn.

"Oh, my God, Fargo," she gasped as he rolled her over and began probing urgently. "Again? I don't know if I can."

"You just lie back and enjoy it," Fargo told her. He was already thrusting, pistonlike, his strokes unhurried and deep. Determined to savor this to the full, he increased his pace only gradually, reveling in each deep, probing exploration of her hot warm pocket. To his surprise, Angelique had forgotten her protest of a moment before and was no longer just lying back and letting him take her. Gradually she began meeting him thrust for thrust, her inner muscles coming alive once more, sucking him in deeper and still deeper.

"Isn't that nice?" she panted.

"Keep it up."

"Feel that!"

Her inner muscles grabbed him deliciously. He almost cried out as he increased his tempo. She flung her arms about his neck and uttered tiny cries of astonished delight as Fargo built himself up to his final explosion. Then his body took over as Angelique, too, went out of control.

Thrashing wildly, she flung herself up violently to meet each of his downward thrusts and came just as Fargo pounded down with a final, brutal stroke. His engorged shaft throbbing almost painfully, he climaxed and kept Angelique impaled beneath him until he was finally and completely drained.

Only then did he release her, and for a while they lay in each other's arms. When the eastern sky began to lighten, she kissed him softly on the lips, then got up and dressed hurriedly. When she was ready to return to the camp, she smiled down at him. He could see the glow in her cheeks as the sky grew brighter.

"I must help Theresa prepare breakfast."

"Don't be in such a hurry," Fargo said. "I'd like a chance to rest up some."

"Why, Fargo, you poor dear, are you all worn out?"

"Don't sneeze. I might blow away."

She laughed lightly, turned, and in a moment had vanished down the slope.

Sighing, Fargo checked his Colt, then closed his eyes for a much-needed catnap. Why was it, he wondered drowsily, that a woman could get so damned active afterward, while a man always felt as if his lifeblood had just been drained completely?

The weaker sex, hell!

7

Two days later, as they were breaking camp, Theresa Wayland hurried over to Fargo, distraught.

"Mister Fargo," she cried, "Sam's run off!"

Fargo was in the act of lacing his bedroll onto his cantle. He glanced sharply at Theresa. "Just slow down, Miss Wayland. "When's the last time you saw him?"

"I was cleaning the pans in the stream. He was helping me. The next time I looked up, he was gone."

"You think he could have been swept away?"

"No. He would have cried out. I would have heard him."

"Then he's wandered off."

"Yes."

Fargo vaulted into his saddle. As he did so, he saw Matthew mounted up also and riding toward him. For an old geezer, he rode straight up, his white hair solid, his dark eyes strong and uncompromising. Pulling to a halt beside Fargo, Matthew said he thought he knew the direction the boy might have taken.

"Lead the way," Fargo said.

They rode downstream, keeping to a broad, grassy sward that followed alongside the stream. It was easy to see how a young boy could be fascinated by such an apparent highway. And at his height he would be invisible in less than ten yards.

The grassy trail came to an abrupt end a half-mile farther on, where a shallow brook emptied into the stream, cutting a deep trench directly across the grassy pathway. They found small footsteps in the mud on the fringes of the creek and in the shallows. They led away from the stream toward higher ground.

"Jesus," Fargo said. "Never knew an eight-year-old could go this far in such a short time."

"I don't like it," Matthew said.

A moment later he pulled up and dismounted, his eyes on the muddy tracks on the ground. His frock coat was torn and soiled and his pants baggy, but it was remarkable how well-dressed Matthew appeared, nevertheless.

"What is it?" Fargo asked.

The old man, mopping his narrow, lined face with a handkerchief, pointed to another set of tracks running parallel with Sam's on the other side of the brook.

They were the tracks of a bear cub.

"That explains why he's making such good time," Fargo said, mounting up quickly.

Matthew nodded grimly as he also stepped into his saddle. "He's been chasing that cub all this time. Probably wants to take him back for a pet."

Fargo nodded and spurred his pinto ahead, growing frantic for some sign of the youngster. If that cub found its mother before they found young Sam, there could be trouble—bad trouble; mother bears were notoriously unpredictable when it came to protecting their young.

They reached a high, pine-studded flat. The brook cut a clean brown swath through the flat. On the other side of the brook, climbing a steep hillside on the far side of the flat, they saw Sam. He was not far behind the cub, and the cub was less than a hundred yards from its mother.

The female reared up on her hind legs as her cub drew closer. Fargo could not tell if the bear had seen Sam yet, but she would in a matter of seconds. Fargo and Matthew spurred their mounts and leapt the brook, galloping across the flat toward the slope. The female bear suddenly roared and began to amble swifly down the slope toward Sam, who stopped hastily, evidently confused by the female's reaction.

Fargo had the sickening sensation they weren't going to reach Sam in time. But just then, already at the base of the slope, another horseman—the trooper Tyler—started up the slope toward Sam. They heard him call out to the boy and saw the boy turn around.

At once Sam ran down the slope toward Tyler,

arms outstretched. Spurring his mount on up the slope toward Sam and the onrushing bear, Tyler reached down and snatched the boy, depositing him on his cantle. Then he wheeled his horse and galloped back down the slope, the mother bear on his heels for a good twenty yards. As soon as Tyler regained the flat, the bear pulled up, watched the horse and rider for a moment, then ambled swiftly back up the slope to see to her cub.

That was when Tyler caught sight of them. Waving his free arm, he turned his horse and galloped toward them. Fargo could see that little Sam was grinning from ear to ear. What sport! he seemed to be saying.

A near-hysterical Theresa took Sam from Tyler. First she smothered him with kisses, then she began spanking the youngster's hide with a tearful fury that must have completely confused him.

As Theresa and Angelique hustled Sam off to their wagon, Matthew dismounted and stood beside Fargo and Tyler.

"Crazy, ain't it?" he said to them. "But that's how a woman shows her concern. Little Sam will understand—someday, if not now."

"I think I understand too," Tyler said. "I remember I ran across a street once and went sprawling in front of a milk truck. My ma ran out and snatched me up a second before the big Percherons would have pounded me into manure. She hugged me all the way back to the sidewalk, then she whaled the tar out of me the rest of the way home."

Matthew looked at the trooper shrewdly. "And I'll bet you went to bed that night without supper."

"Yup," Tyler said, grinning.

"Tyler," Fargo said, "you came out of nowhere back there. How'd you find us?"

"I followed you from the timber above the stream. I figured I could cover the ground you'd be missing from up there. I was pretty sure Sam hadn't crossed to the other side of the stream."

"Well, it's a good thing you showed up when you did," said Matthew. "We might not have reached the boy in time if you hadn't."

"Yeah," said Fargo, clapping the trooper on the back.

Tyler nodded, acknowledging their praise with a slightly embarrassed shrug . He looked at Fargo. "You want the same formation as yesterday?" the trooper asked.

"Why not?"

"Foster's been complainin' about always riding drag."

"You want it?"

"I don't mind, Mister Fargo."

"Tell Foster."

Tyler hurried off to where the three troopers had gathered. Watching him go, Matthew remarked that Tyler was the best of the lot. Fargo agreed.

Then he saw Crow Woman standing by the other wagon, her face impassive. She beckoned to him. Fargo left Matthew and walked over to her.

"Fargo not forget?"

"My promise to take you to your people?"

"Yes."

"I haven't forgotten."

"I come to you tonight."

"You think I won't keep my promise if you don't?"

There was sudden merriment in her dark, lustrous eyes. "I take no chance. I not want you to forget Crow Woman."

"Ain't no likelihood of that."

"I see you tonight."

Fargo shrugged. She turned and left him.

Though he tried not to show it, the thought of her working him over raised his heartbeat a couple of beats. If Angelique started hinting around, he would just have to tell her he was going to check the watch, or that he had a headache. She wouldn't believe him, of course, but so what? He chuckled. It sure was hell on wheels escorting unattached females through the wilderness.

Later that same afternoon, Fargo heard hooves pounding toward him and turned in his saddle. It was Tyler. The trooper seemed agitated.

Fargo pulled to a halt and waited for Tyler to reach him. As he did so, the two wagons continued on past him. Jeb and Angelique, each driving a wagon, waved to him as they passed. Fargo waved back. Sam and Beth, sitting in the last wagon, peered out at him from the rear opening and waved too. Sam was a much more sober young man as a result of his morning walk, and Beth too seemed uncommonly solemn. This was sure as hell not an easy journey for kids, Fargo reflected.

Matthew and Crow Woman were riding alongside each other. The old man saluted casually as
he passed Fargo. Crow Woman watched him sidelong with her luminous, almond-shaped eyes and
Fargo wondered what mischief was simmering
between the old man and the Indian woman. If it
was what he thought it was, he wished the old
man luck.

Tyler pulled up alongside of him.

"What's the problem?" Fargo asked.

"I'm not sure. We might have visitors."

"Sioux?"

"I'm not sure."

Fargo did not want to believe Black Feather
would have followed them this far. But perhaps
the chief's appetite for bluecoat scalps had not
been sated by those renegades Fargo had left at
the fort.

"Let's go," Fargo said.

They rode back along the trail at a full gallop
until they were out of sight of the wagons.
Abruptly, Tyler pulled up. Fargo reined his pinto
and looked back at him.

"What the hell?"

"I have to talk fast," Tyler explained.

"Then do it."

"There's no Indians. The rest of the troopers
want your hide. Hennessey's behind it, and I'm
supposed to bring you to them."

"You mean they don't want to go on to Fort
Laramie?"

Tyler nodded briskly. "And they want the
three women."

"They think you're in this with them?"

"Yes."

"But you ain't?"

"I couldn't do it. Not to them kids—and the others."

"You must have a plan."

"They're supposed to come down on both sides with one of them in front, so you won't bolt. And I'm supposed to pull back and cover you from the rear. But I figure if we can make them think you're going along, maybe we can shoot fast enough to take them."

"That's a big maybe. There's only two of us and there's three of them."

"I'd wait for you to make your move, then I'd back you."

Fargo nodded. He was taking a chance Tyler was on the level. But he saw no reason for the man to make all this up and decided his only course was to trust him.

"Let's move out, then," Fargo said. "They see us talkin' like this, they'll suspect something. Where are they supposed to meet us?"

"Over that next hogback, where the trail winds through some timber."

Fargo remembered riding through it earlier. He nudged his pinto and quickly lifted it to a lope.

As they neared the hogback, Fargo took his Colt out of its holster, thumb-cocked it, and stuck it down his back, between his heavy buckskin jacket and his shirt—and high enough so he could grab the butt with one quick reach. Then he leaned over and checked the load on his Sharps, took off the safety, and eased it up a little out of the scabbard. The last thing he did before he topped the hogback was pull the fringed skirt of his buckskin jacket forward over his empty holster.

They were well into the timber when the three troopers materialized from the woods just as Tyler had predicted. One swept down from the right, the other from the left, while the third trooper pulled his chestnut to a halt in front of them. This was Hennessey, and he had his Colt out and a nasty grin on his face.

Fargo pulled up obediently as Tyler took out his Colt and covered Fargo from the rear. Fargo tied his reins about the saddle horn and raised his hands. He did a good job of showing both astonishment and anger at this apparent betrayal.

"You fools," he said. "You do this and you'll never be able to square yourself with the army."

"The hell with the army," said Ned, the trooper to Fargo's left.

Hennessey cocked his revolver. "And to hell with you too, Fargo. You took us out of trouble, sure enough. Now it's time for us to make our move."

"And get our reward," said the third trooper, the one on Fargo's right. He laughed then, a wet, sniveling laugh that sounded as if he were blowing his nose.

Fargo glanced at him and started to lower his hands.

"Keep them hands high," said Hennessey.

Fargo raised his hands again, a little higher than before, his right hand drifting back a little.

"Ned," said Hennessey, "pull the son of a bitch's Colt out of his holster and hand it here."

"Hey, I want it!"

"You can have his Sharps."

Ned liked that. His eyes gleamed as he holstered his own weapon and leaned over to flip back Fargo's buckskin jacket to get at Fargo's Colt.

As soon as Ned's fingers closed about the jacket, Fargo spurred his pinto forward, his right hand dipping back for the Colt. As he pulled out the gun and charged the astonished Hennessey, the trooper got off one wild shot, wheeled his horse, and fled before Fargo.

Glancing to his right, Fargo saw Ned tugging on his revolver. But he was already too late. Fargo's six-gun belched fire. Ned's right eyeball vanished and the back of his head splattered the trees behind him as he was flung backward off his horse. At the same time came an explosion from behind Fargo. Looking back, Fargo saw the third trooper go tumbling sideways off his horse.

Tyler, a smoking six-gun in his hand, watched the trooper thud to the ground, his face ashen. As the dead trooper lay spread-eagle on his back, staring sightlessly up at Tyler, Fargo thought Tyler was going to get sick.

"First time you ever kill a man?"

Tyler nodded.

"Well, it was in a good cause."

"What now?"

"Go back to the wagons. Keep a sharp eye out. I'm going after Hennessey."

Tyler nodded and turned his horse. Fargo watched him go, then glanced down at the two dead troopers. Food for buzzards. Undoubtedly the best use they had ever been put to during their entire lives.

Clapping his heels to his pinto, Fargo took off after Hennessey.

An hour or so before sundown, Fargo overtook the fleeing trooper. Hennessey had made no effort to hide his tracks or to pull up and make any kind of a stand. Only with his horse close to giving out on him, did he dismount and fling himself facedown.

All this Fargo read in the man's tracks as he dismounted in the timber above him. Tethering his Ovaro, Fargo picked his way carefully down the slope toward the exhausted trooper. Hennessey was making so much noise as he drank that he did not hear Fargo leave the brush and walk across the narrow clearing toward him.

Fargo was less than five feet from Hennessey when he heard a guttural voice come from the other side of the stream. A second later he saw the head of a paint emerge from behind a thin line of birch and willow, and after that came the stealthy figure of a Sioux brave, his eyes studying intently the trail before him.

In front of Fargo, Hennessey looked up, startled. Fargo flung himself through the air, hitting the trooper so hard that he sagged forward into the water barely conscious. Clasping one hand around the trooper's mouth, Fargo dragged the dazed man into a thick clump of alder. Then, holding the struggling man as firmly as he could, Fargo watched the Sioux emerge from the timber on the other side of the stream. Hennessey's horse, still saddled, was out of sight farther down in the alders, drinking from the stream. Fargo knew that as soon as Hennessey's horse got wind of the Indian ponies on the other bank, it would raise its head and whicker.

Fargo dragged the trooper through the brush and up the slope toward his tethered Ovaro. It was not easy. Hennessey seemed more terrified of Fargo than he did of the Sioux. As Fargo dragged the trooper along, he glanced down at the stream. Two, then three Sioux were splashing across it now, heading for Hennessey's horse. One of the Sioux was giving instructions to the other Sioux to fan out, look around. They knew the owner of this army horse must be close by.

Fargo moved more swiftly up the slope, exerting every ounce of his energy in an effort to keep the terrified trooper from breaking loose and running, half-crazed, back into the arms of the Sioux. At last, unable to quiet the man, Fargo grimly wrestled him to the ground, his right palm still over his mouth. As Hennessey tried to bite through his left palm, Fargo took out his Colt and with his right hand pressed the length of the barrel against the trooper's windpipe.

Hennessey died hard, his fingers tearing desperately at the gun barrel as it slowly crushed the life out of him. At last, his eyes bulging, his swollen tongue protruding obscenely from his mouth, Hennessey arched his back and gave up the ghost.

Just in time.

A shadow fell over Fargo a second before the Indian's foot crushed a twig behind him. Whirling, Fargo reached back for his bowie just as the Sioux's war club whooshed down. It missed the back of Fargo's head, but crunched painfully into the fleshy part of his shoulder. Anxious not to make a sound and draw any more Sioux, Fargo rolled over swiftly one more time, then came up on all fours. The Sioux, off balance from swinging his war club, hesitated just an instant.

Fargo charged, keeping his shoulder low. His head caught the Sioux in the gut, bowling him back. Before the savage could gasp or cry out, Fargo closed one hand over his mouth and with the other dug the bowie deep into the Indian's bowels. Twisting it upward, Fargo withdrew the blade just under the brave's rib cage.

Wiping the blade off on the Sioux's leggings, Fargo looked back down the slope. The clearing was filled with Sioux, as was the other side of the stream. It was a sizable war party and appeared to be making camp for the night. Peering intently down at them, Fargo eventually caught sight of Black Feather.

Black Feather's appetite, it seemed, was still healthy. He wanted more bluecoats—and he wanted Fargo and the others as well. Then Fargo thought of Crow Woman. Hell! It was more than that. The horny old bastard was after Crow Woman as well.

Fargo dragged over the dead trooper and dumped him on top of the dead Indian. Then he took the Indian's knife, placed it in the trooper's right hand, after which he tightened the dead Sioux's fingers around the trooper's throat. Standing back, Fargo surveyed his grisly handiwork. It looked at first glimpse as if both men had died killing each other. If the Sioux didn't look too closely, it just might prevent them from looking for a third party.

Fargo found his pinto and led it swiftly through the thick timber for almost a quarter of a mile before mounting up and riding off. The way he figured it, the Sioux were less than a day behind them. But they could easily be a hell of a lot closer if they figured out what really happened back there with that Sioux and the trooper.

As dusk closed over the landscape, Fargo urged his surefooted beast to greater speed.

8

Fargo overtook the wagons early the next morning.

Seeing him coming, Tyler peeled away from the wagons and rode back to meet him. Tyler seemed to have taken charge nicely, judging from the way he indicated to Jeb and Matthew to stay with the wagons. Fargo was pleased to see little Beth and Sam, safe and sound, shading their eyes and peering at him from the rear of the second wagon.

"Did you get Hennessey?" Tyler shouted, pulling up and swinging his horse around to accompany Fargo.

Fargo nodded.

"He's dead?"

"I'm here, ain't I?"

"A stupid question. Sorry."

"Forget it. We got other troubles."

"Indians?"

"Sioux. Black Feather."

"Jesus, ain't we seen the last of that bastard?"

"Don't look like it."

"How far back is he?"

"Half a day's ride, I'd say."

"So what do we do?"

"Keep moving—only faster. No stops except to rest and feed the horses."

"What about the women and the two kids?"

"Tyler, I told you. We got to move fast or there won't be women or kids to worry about."

"How soon before Black Feather catches up with us?"

"Before we're ready, more than likely."

"Yeah. That means we fight."

"That's what it means. Now, go tell the others. I want to talk to Crow Woman."

They had almost reached the wagons by then. As Tyler lifted his horse to a lope to overtake Theresa Wayland's wagon, it was obvious she and Tyler were fast becoming more than friends. Jeb glanced around from his seat on the second wagon and waved to Fargo. Fargo waved back, then rode over toward Crow Woman.

She had been riding alongside Matthew until she saw him coming. She pulled up, letting Matthew ride on ahead.

"Keep riding," Fargo told her, pulling his pinto alongside her mount.

"You kill trooper?" she asked, starting up again.

"That ain't what I want to talk about."

She shrugged and kept riding.

117

"Black Feather is on our backs, still coming after us. I'm wondering why he wants us so bad. And the only answer I'm comin' up with is you. He wants you back."

"And so now you want to give me back to him so you can go free. Like you do with the bluecoats."

"No, dammit! That ain't what I want."

She glanced at him for a long moment, apparently deciding whether or not to believe him. Then she spoke. "Chief Black Feather call me whore and send me to Fargo's lodge to punish me. Now I leave the chief to his own woman. She is old and her tongue is sharp. She is good only to gather wood. You are right, Skye. I know what you say is true. Old bulls like fresh grass. Black Feather comes after Crow Woman. But she will die before she sleep in his lodge again."

"Maybe we all will," Fargo noted coldly.

Crow woman shrugged. "Does Skye Fargo's heart beat like frightened animal?"

"Yes, I am afraid, Crow Woman. But not for myself."

She nodded, as if she understood perfectly. "Yes. Fargo has much fear for the others. The two white women. The little ones and the old man with snow in his hair and fire in his blood. Crow Woman has fear for them too. But she will not go back to Chief Black Feather." She glanced sidelong at Fargo. "I go back to my people now. And you will take me there. Is that not so, Skye?"

Fargo nodded. "I gave you my word."

"Crow Woman see how you are with this Angelique, so she think it might be you leave her behind for the old chief. But now I know Skye Fargo not speak with forked tongue. Crow Woman speak no more of this."

With that, Crow Woman urged her pony to a lope and left Fargo behind. He watched her for a moment, then with a sigh increased his pace until he came alongside Jeb's wagon. Reaching out with one hand, he grabbed the canvas framing and swung onto the seat beside Jeb.

"I just heard," Jeb said, spitting out a long black dart of tobacco. "We got company comin'."

"Which means we better set the table—and fast."

"I'm listening."

"I figure our best bet is to keep an eye out for a good spot, one we can defend. You know these redskins. They don't like any drawn-out battles."

Jeb spat out another gob of tobacco juice. "That's right. They can't afford big losses. Their women don't give them enough sons, not by a long shot."

"So we keep a sharp lookout."

"And someone better drop back to let us know if Black Feather's gettin' any closer."

"I'll do that."

Fargo leaned back on the seat, needing a few minutes to get his bearings. He felt a tap on his shoulder, turned, and saw Angelique.

"I was resting back here," she said, "and heard. Can I help?"

"Sure. Sit up here with Jeb—and stay alert."

She glanced at Jeb's back and winked at Fargo. "That won't be so hard," she said.

A few moments later, as Fargo remounted and started back to cover the rear, he saw Angelique climbing onto the seat beside Jeb. She seemed right at home beside the old mountain man.

Later that day, riding after the wagons through a narrow pass, Fargo caught sight of what he realized might turn out to be the natural fortress he had been hoping to find. It was a high escarpment, a sheer wall of rock that stared down at him like a vast, broken face. On a steep ridge at the base of the cliff sat great boulders, some as large as houses, all of them offering excellent protection from any assault from below. Once established upon that ridge, Fargo realized, it would be almost impossible for the Sioux to storm it successfully.

He called out to Tyler, indicating the trooper should hold up the wagons.

As the wagons slowed, then halted, Fargo turned his pinto off the trail and rode closer to the escarpment to study the ridge below the cliff. The slope leading up to the ridge was steep enough, but negotiable—and it would sure as hell prove a problem to any attacking Sioux.

Fargo rode back onto the trail and back to the wagons.

Tyler had dismounted and he and Jeb were waiting beside the halted wagons for him, while Matthew and Crow Woman remained mounted, content to let the three men decide things.

Pulling up beside Jeb and Tyler, Fargo dismounted.

"You thinkin' what I'm thinkin'?" asked Jeb, indicating the escarpment with a nod of his head.

120

"I figure we could hold off an army from that ridge."

"How many rounds do we have?"

"Enough, more than enough. And plenty of weapons."

"Water?"

"Way ahead of you. We got six barrels in the lead wagon."

"Counting Matthew," Fargo reminded Jeb, "there's only the four of us, don't forget. Unless we can count on the women."

"That ain't such a crazy idea, Fargo. Not if yer thinkin' of Angelique."

"You think she can handle a gun that good?"

"Do bears shit in the woods? She was the one helped me beat off Blaine and the troopers when they raided the wagons back at the fort. Them bastards would have taken everything. If it hadn't been for her, they would've."

"What about Theresa?"

"I figure that with Tyler as a steadying influence, she might be able to keep his rifle loaded."

Fargo nodded. It wasn't much, perhaps, but it was the best they could count on. "And I got a feeling Crow Woman might be some help, too."

Crow Woman suddenly called out, "Fargo!"

He looked up at her and saw she was pointing back to the pass. Fargo followed her gaze and swore. Tyler and Jeb swore also. Black Feather and his war party were streaming through the pass toward them. The Sioux had already sighted them, and even from that distance they could all hear the Sioux's war cries.

Fargo stepped up into his saddle. "Get these wagons headin' for that ridge," Fargo cried to Jeb and Tyler. "It's steep enough, but you can make it."

Jeb jumped up onto the lead wagon's seat, taking the reins from Theresa Wayland, and whipped the horses toward the slope at a quick gallop. Tyler mounted his horse, spun around, took the bridle of Angelique's lead horse, and began pulling it up the slope. Angelique stood up and slapped the reins, letting out a shrill, blood-curdling yell that sent her team charging up the slope after the first wagon. Tyler let go of the bridle and allowed the wagon to sweep on past him up the slope.

By the time Fargo and Tyler overtook the wagons, the Sioux were strung out in a long line, galloping swiftly toward the slope. As Fargo charged past the second wagon, he could hear the frightened cries of the two children inside as they hung on grimly to the lurching, steeply climbing wagon. Fargo wanted to look in to make sure they were all right, but realized he did not have the time.

Once he reached the ridge ahead of the wagons, Fargo dismounted, found a boulder to set up behind, and with his Sharps and Colt began pouring fire down upon the first rank of Sioux charging up the slope. His fire cut a few ponies out from under the warriors, and that was enough to create some disarray in their ranks. A second later Tyler was at his side, loading his Hawken.

"Aim low," Fargo told him. "For their mounts!"

122

Tyler nodded and commenced firing. In a few seconds, their combined fire caused the Sioux to wheel their mounts and charge back down the slope.

"I'll stay here," Fargo told Tyler. "You go on back and get those wagons hid proper near the base of the cliff. I'll join you later."

"You don't want to make a stand here?"

Fargo looked quickly around him at the terrain. "No. This spot is too exposed."

Tyler mounted up and galloped after the wagons, disappearing behind the boulders.

Looking back down the slope, Fargo saw a group of bloodthirsty Sioux huddled in an impromptu war council. Some were gesticulating and others were obviously trying to get the more hot-tempered among them to calm down. Fargo watched them for a moment, a demonic light growing in his eyes.

Steadying his Sharps on the boulder in front of him, Fargo made a telescope out of his hand and peered for a moment at the group of Indians to get some estimate of the distance between him and the palavering Indians. He figured it to be close to four hundred yards. He adjusted the rifle's sights, after which, frowning in concentration, he lifted the barrel about half an inch and aimed for one of the most excitable of the Indians, a tall Sioux with a resplendent war bonnet. Swallowing carefully, he took a deep breath, then squeezed the trigger gently.

As the crash of the Sharp's powerful blast exploded on the slopes around him, Fargo waited, not expecting much. Abruptly, the knot of Indians suddenly broke up in disarray as the tall Indian dropped to the ground. It had been one helluva lucky shot, Fargo realized with grim satisfaction, but one a Sharps made more often than most.

Fargo pulled out then, mounting up and galloping back into the rocks to help set up their defensive perimeter. It was getting late in the day and he expected Black Feather to make one all-out attack by dusk at the latest.

As Fargo expected, the next attack came at dusk and was led off by a foolish brave determined to gain renown. He rose out of a clump of bunch grass about fifty yards in front of Fargo's position, flung his lance, then dashed toward Fargo, firing a big navy Colt as he came. He got as far as the rocks before Fargo planted a black hole in his bare, gleaming chest. And still the crazed brave kept right on coming.

As swiftly as he could, Fargo reloaded and brought his rifle up a second time. The Indian was less than twenty yards from him now, staggering drunkenly, but still coming. Fargo fired, his round slapping into the brave's left side, spinning him around. Even this did not stop the Indian. Once he was facing Fargo again, he lowered his head and plunged toward him. Fargo dropped the Sharps and was reaching for his Colt when Jeb shot the brave in the head.

That did it. Like an oversized Christmas toy winding down, the garishly painted Indian spun blindly to the ground.

Fargo glanced over at Jeb in time to see another brave darting from behind another boulder, this one heading for the trapper. Fargo tracked him quickly and squeezed off a shot. A sudden freshet of blood erupted from the Sioux's throat.

Those two frontal attacks were the signal for the attack to begin as up and down the ridge line, the Sioux, no longer mounted, charged through the rocks toward the wagons.

Farther down, Tyler's firing was almost continuous, and the next time Fargo glanced over at Jeb, he saw Angelique beside him firing steadily with one of the army rifles, her shoulder taking the recoil with the ease of a man twice her weight. Jeb was firing and reloading with a speed that rivaled Fargo's own handling of the Sharps.

As the Indians got closer, Fargo resorted to his Colt and Jeb to his huge Walker. Then Fargo heard someone moving up beside him. He glanced over to see Crow Woman, her dark eyes alight with excitement as she took a place alongside Fargo and proceeded to fire an army rifle steadily at the onrushing Sioux. Like Angelique, she seemed to have no difficulty at all with the recoil. Farther down, old Matthew, with Theresa beside him to reload his rifle, was also banging away with considerable effect.

The slaughter went on for at least ten minutes without one Sioux getting any closer to their lines than that Sioux warrior who had led off the attack. Gradually, the Indians began pulling out, dragging their dead after them.

Fargo looked down the line and his gaze was

met by nervous but hopeful faces. Tyler waved. Fargo waved back. Matthew doffed his black hat.

"What do you think, Fargo?" Jeb called.

"I don't trust the bastards."

Jeb smiled and nodded. His sentiments exactly.

Fargo glanced at Crow Woman. "You did well back there, Crow Woman. I guess maybe you don't really want to go back with Chief Black Feather."

"I tell you before. He is old. With him a woman must work too hard to please him. His juices are gone."

Fargo got the picture. The poor son of a bitch. He almost felt sorry for him. He glanced about him again. The Indians were lying low now, not a sound coming from behind the rocks. Fargo remained uneasy.

Suddenly a chill fell over him. Where were the two kids? he asked himself as he looked back at the wagons. They were lost in the gloom of a huge boulder, but the second wagon, where the two kids had been left, was almost entirely visible and Fargo could see it clearly.

The kids were supposed to be in that second wagon, and they were probably there still, huddled in each other's arms. Yet the firing was over, the cries of the attacking Sioux no longer filled the air. Why weren't they calling out? Or at least peering out of the back of the wagon as they usually did? Were they really that terrified?

Fargo left Crow Woman and hurried back to the wagons. He was almost to the second wagon when he saw a Sioux cautiously sticking his head out of the rear opening in the canvas. At the sight of

Fargo, the brave dived free of the wagon, holding the unconscious Beth under one arm like a sack of grain. Behind this one came another brave, little Sam under his arm.

Fargo dared not shoot for fear of hitting the children. Instead he flung himself at both braves before they could recover their balance, driving the two Indians into each other. The first Sioux dropped Beth. The other one abandoned Sam and drew his knife. Fargo fired from his hip, catching him in the gut. Turning back to the first Indian, he saw the brave was almost on him, his blade upraised.

An army rifle thundered on his left, and the Indian, half of his head blown away, crumpled forward. Fargo stepped out of his way to let the dead brave fall to the ground. Turning, he saw Crow Woman slowly lowering her rifle.

Theresa must have seen Fargo racing back to the wagons. She was in their midst now, reaching for the children, clutching them to her, crying frantically, half beside herself with concern. Both children had been struck blows on the head. Blood was running down their necks and faces, but as Theresa wrapped them to her, they both came alive with a vengeance and began screaming with terror.

Though he winced at the clamor, never had Fargo heard such a welcome racket. With lungs like that, it was clear they were both still healthy, even if they were banged up some.

"They'll be all right," Fargo told Theresa. "Get them back into the wagon and see to those wounds. Stay in there with them. Matt can load his rifle without your help."

Still hugging the two sobbing children to her, tears streaming down her own face, Theresa nodded gratefully. Gathering up the two, she lifted them into the wagon and climbed in after them.

Fargo turned to Crow Woman. "You saved my life."

She smiled. "Black Feather lose many braves." She pointed to one of the dead Sioux, the brave she had brought down with her rifle. "That one. He is Gold Eagle, son of Black Feather. How many Black Feather pull back. Already he lose too much."

"Maybe. But I wouldn't count on it."

She shrugged. "It does not matter. Already we are close to my people. Soon they will find us—and the Sioux."

"I hope you're right, Crow Woman."

A little later, waiting for the Sioux to come at them again, Fargo convened an informal war council in front of the wagons.

"I think we better split up," Fargo told them.

"Split up?" Tyler asked.

"That's right. You, me, and Jeb take positions closer to the rocks and station the others back here in the wagons." Fargo looked at Matthew. "That means you, too, Matt."

The old man shrugged. "Whatever you say, Fargo."

"Why do you want us to stay back here?" Angelique asked. "I can fire as well as any man."

"Hell, that's what I'm counting on. If we get driven back to the wagons, with you and the others here it will mean there'll be some firepower waiting to cover us. And we should have someone back here anyway, just in case. Look at what almost happened to the kids."

Theresa nodded quickly. It was obvious she agreed heartily.

"That means we'll be spread pretty thin out there," Jeb observed.

Fargo looked at him. "You got a better plan?"

"Nope."

"Then it's settled."

Tyler said, "Now, all we got to do is wait for them bastards to try again. When do you think they will?"

Jeb scratched his bewhiskered face. "I'm thinking it'll be just before dawn."

"That's the way I see it," Fargo said. He looked at the women. "I suggest you all try to get some sleep."

"What about you?" asked Angelique.

Fargo shrugged. He planned to get plenty of sleep after they finished with Black Feather—if they finished him, that is. But right now, staying awake was more important than sleep, unless he wanted to take that other, longer sleep.

For the rest of that night, Jeb, and Tyler waited for Black Feather to renew the attack. But Jeb had called it. Not until it was nearly dawn did the attack come.

Out of the gloom, two braves led the assault on

Fargo's position. Fargo stopped one with his Sharps, then resorted to his Colt, catching the second one high enough in the chest to send him reeling back. As Fargo reloaded his Sharps, he saw Tyler picking off an Indian who had climbed one of the boulders and was shooting down at them from it. Jeb, too, was firing coolly on the swarm of skulking shapes materializing in front of his position, and he was making each shot count. In a matter of minutes, the Indians lost heart and melted back into the predawn shadows, but they kept up a steady fire. Tyler and Jeb both suffered minor flesh wounds, neither injury enough to take either man out of the line.

When the first gray rays of the morning sun poked over the horizon, there was a momentary lull in the fire, which told Fargo to expect some kind of flanking attack. He relayed his apprehensions down the line. The first sign that Fargo had called it right was when he heard the heel of a moccasin strike the surface of a rock close behind him. Swinging his Colt around, he fired up at the figure hurtling through the air. The sweating, stinking body struck him a numbing blow, knocking his Colt out of his hand.

As Fargo flung the lifeless Indian off him, another brave leapt at him. There was no time for Fargo to retrieve his Colt. Unsheathing his bowie, he warded off the brave's war club and with his right hand drove the bowie hilt deep into the brave's side. He heard the Indian gasp, and as he withdrew the blade, he was drenched in the sudden warm gout of blood that erupted from the savage's side.

Ignoring the hot blood soaking his shirt and britches, Fargo flung the dead brave from him and, turning, saw a powerful Sioux coming up on Jeb from behind, his knife upraised. Jeb was busy firing at two warriors coming at him from the rocks.

"Jeb!" Fargo cried. "Behind you!"

Jeb whirled as Fargo snatched up his Colt and fired from a kneeling position. The slug found its mark and the Indian jackknifed, then stumbled drunkenly past Jeb's position. He kept going until he tripped over a body and sprawled facedown in the dust.

"Move back," Fargo cried. He sheathed his knife and picked up his Sharps. "To the wagons!"

Jeb and Tyler left their positions and dashed up the slight incline that led to the wagons—Fargo, close behind them, firing back at the Indians as he went. As the three men neared the wagons, a sudden explosion of rapid fire coming from the wagons cut down at least two more braves.

Once in the cover of the wagons, Fargo noted that Angelique's rifle was almost as devastating as Matthew's—as she had insisted earlier.

The battle raged for a half-hour longer as each of the defenders went from one rifle to another, so hot did each piece become. Only a few of Black Feather's braves managed to break through their fire and reach the wagons. And in each case they were cut down with savage fury, Crow Woman and Angelique as deadly as the men.

Somehow a brave managed to work his way to the rear of the wagons by creeping along the rock face. It was Theresa who discovered him. She was inside the wagon with the kids and was not armed except for a small hatchet they used for cutting firewood. As the brave skulked closer to the defenders, Theresa leaned out of the wagon behind him and sank the blade of the ax between his ears. The Indian uttered not a sound as he toppled to the ground, the blade still firmly planted in his skull.

Fargo looked into the wagon after they dragged away the Indian. Theresa was sitting in the corner of the wagon, hugging both children to her, her face stony, her eyes staring straight ahead. Fargo climbed into the wagon and spoke to her softly. For a frightening moment he thought she was not aware of his presence, but then she acknowledged him with a weary glance and he saw two tears move down her cheeks. She was going to be all right.

After this attempt at infiltration, the Indians pulled back. But the lull did not fool Fargo nor Jeb, and soon enough, from out of the rocks came a barrage of flaming arrows. In a moment the canvas on the wagons was burning furiously. But using more than any of them would have wished of their precious water, they soon had the flames out.

While they were struggling with this new threat, Black Feather sent one more wave of braves. And this time Fargo saw what he had been hoping for since the attack began: the old chief himself.

"Get Black Feather," he cried to the others, pointing.

At once the old chief found himself under intense fire. A second later, a slug caught him in the leg and he went down. Braves dragged him out of the line of fire, then carried him off.

Almost immediately the Indians' fire petered out and ceased. Fargo glimpsed some braves hauling off their wounded. This battle was over.

Fargo waited a decent interval, then crept out from behind the wagons and into the rocks. Once through them, he looked down the slope and saw the remnants of Black Feather's war party gathering around the old chief, who was leaning painfully against his pony. There seemed to be an argument going on, and Fargo had a pretty good idea what they were arguing about.

There were a lot fewer braves now than when Black Feather first led them through that pass the day before. Ten braves, at least, were gone—a significant number for any attacking war party to lose. Losses of this dimension would turn the chief's village into a wailing babble of morning men and women, some of them deliberately maiming themselves in their grief.

Old Black Feather had been foolish to press so recklessly his attack on Fargo's nearly impregnable position. And all because of his desire for Crow Woman. Fargo chuckled grimly to himself. There sure as hell was no fool like an old fool.

Fargo noticed that Crow Woman was beside him.

"What the hell're you doin' out here?" Fargo demanded.

"I come to see the old one who come after me. Is he dead?"

"Just a scratch, looks like."

"He is very foolish chief. He should go back to his people now. Many fine braves he lose."

One of the braves slipped onto a pony. Fargo saw the others crowding around while Black Feather gave the mounted brave last-minute instructions. Then Black Feather stepped back, favoring his leg, and waved good-bye to the mounted warrior.

The warrior lashed his pony to a gallop and headed for the pass.

"Yes," said Crow Woman, "Black Feather is a fool. He send for more braves."

"You sure of that?"

She looked at him as if he had horseshit for brains. "Does the chief not stay with his braves? Does he not send brave back to Sioux camp? Black Feather know you are trapped where you are now. He will wait. He cannot go back to his village without your scalps. Not now."

"And he can't go back without you."

"Yes. He must have me, too. He will make me walk back. He will tie my hands behind my back. He will hold the rope that binds me and many times I will fall and each time he will drag me to my feet. This is what he will do. Black Feather cannot go back to his people with nothing."

Fargo nodded. He understood perfectly. Like a big man in town who has already dropped more than he could afford, Black Feather's only recourse now was to stay in the game until he could recoup his losses—or put a bullet through his head.

"I think maybe now you listen to Crow Woman."

"I'm listening."

"Crow Woman and Fargo, they leave now and go find Crow Woman's people. They will return and take the scalps of these foolish Sioux. It will be a great victory. Old men will sing of it through many winters."

"You so sure we'll be able to find your people?"

Her eyes grew larger and seemed to glow. "Already we are in Crow country now. I can feel it."

"When do we leave?"

"Now."

Fargo slipped cautiously back through the rocks with Crow Woman. They had to find help, Fargo reckoned, and fast. Yet, he was uneasy at the prospect of leaving Jeb and the others behind while he and Crow Woman went searching for her People.

Still, Crow Woman was right.

They were trapped on that ridge and could not hold out forever. Fargo had hoped he could inflict enough casualties on the Sioux war party to make Black Feather pull out. He hadn't counted on

Black Feather being so determined—or so horny, for that matter.

The way it looked now, only the Crows could pull this particular chestnut out of the fire for him—and only if Crow Woman could convince them to help.

9

Slipping away under cover of darkness was a ticklish business. They wrapped their horses' hooves in bucksin and kept their hands over the animals' snouts to prevent them from whickering as they passed close by the Sioux horse herd. But Crow Woman moved as swiftly and as silently through the dark night as Fargo, and soon they mounted and moved off at a fine clip.

When drawn broke, they were many miles from the wagons, and Crow Woman was looking about her eagerly, as if she expected to see her Crow tribesmen materializing from every clump of birch or stand of pine. Fargo was still uneasy about leaving them all back there. His only consolation was that they were well provisioned and there was still an abundance of water. But the most important element in their favor was Jeb. He was a tough old fighter from way back, with more tricks up his sleeve than a grandfather coyote. If anyone could pull them through, Jeb Dugan could.

When they set out, Crow Woman had assured Fargo they would find her people within a day's journey, if not sooner. But two days passed and not a single Indian popped out of the bush. They saw no smoke on the horizon and found no prints around streams. They came upon the abandoned sites of two Indian villages, but the dog turds had long since turned to solid rock.

On the third night, Fargo was too restless to sleep. Crow Woman had said nothing when he suggested they bed down separately. But when a little after midnight he sat up, hugging his knees, gazing back the way he had come, she rose from her pine boughs and walked over to him. She was stark-naked.

The moon was sitting high overhead, shedding enough light for him to see the dark triangle where her long thighs met. Her round belly and taut, melonlike breasts gleamed palely.

"Fargo cannot sleep."

"Where's them people of yours?"

"Soon we find."

"Yeah. You said that yesterday."

"Go back to your friend Jeb. I will find my people and bring them to you."

He looked at her, wondering if he could trust her. Shit. Could any man trust any woman, ever? Still, what choice did he have?

"All right," he told her. "I'll go back tomorrow."

She knelt before him and smiled. "Now I make

you sleep." She reached out and pulled him to her.

He suddenly found himself kissing her as hungrily as she was kissing him. He realized then how much he had wanted her ever since they left the wagons. He pulled her around until she was on his blanket, then flung himself onto her, his tongue probing deeply, hungrily. When he drew back finally, she lifted her head and fastened her teeth about his upper lip and pulled him back down, spreading her legs at the same time.

She was ready. More than ready. He could feel the hot moist warmth of her muff when he reached down. Then her strong fingers were closing about his erection as she thrust her thighs up with an almost angry urgency—as if his delay in taking her these past two nights had made her resentful. He felt himself plunging into her, going so deep he could feel the tip of his erection strike bottom.

She cried out and thrust her thighs up still higher, then wrapped both legs around his waist, gasping in pleasure. He felt the muscles of her vagina grabbing, then holding him as he continued his wild, battering thrusting. The mindless rhythm of it took hold and soon they were whaling away at each other like two kids. She began flinging her head from side to side, her eyes shut tightly, swearing steadily in a mixture of Crow and what sounded like Spanish. The savage sound of it sent a delicious shiver up Fargo's spine.

That was what did it for him.

With a sudden, grim plunge he drove down into

her, impaling her with a ferocity that matched her own. He felt her shudder under him as she let out a prolonged scream that was more like a wail of terror than pleasure. It sent shock waves of desire through him and he began to come repeatedly, clinging to her fiercely as climaxes convulsed them both. They grew into each other, becoming one flesh, a single, twisting, moaning entity . . .

Crow Woman did not go back to her blanket that night, and before the moon traveled much farther across the sky, Fargo was sleeping like a rock.

As Fargo finished saddling his pinto and reached for his bedroll the next morning, he heard the dim thunder of unshod hooves. Looking up, he found his camp encircled by handsome, brightly clad Indians. One look at the high pompadours on their heads and their long braids tied with strips of otter skin, and Fargo knew they had at last found Crow Woman's people.

They seemed friendly enough, but they remained astride their ponies, eyeing both Fargo and Crow Woman coldly. It dawned on Fargo then that though these redskins might be Crows, it didn't necessarily mean they were Crow Woman's people. She might have come from another band.

One of the braves kneed his pony closer to Fargo's Ovaro, his eyes gleaming as he looked it over from nose to tail. Fargo could tell that it would not take much of an excuse for the Crow to send a shaft through his heart so that he could claim the handsome pinto and stake it outside his lodge. The brave's face hardened in resolve suddenly and he nudged his own pony still closer, attempting to wedge himself between Fargo and the pinto. Fargo felt his own blood rising. He was in no position to take on this brave, but he sure as hell had not ridden this far and for this long to have some dandified redskin take away his Ovaro.

He drew his Colt and grabbed the halter of the Indian's pony. Thumb-cocking the Colt, he aimed it up at the Crow.

"Move back, you son of a bitch," Fargo told him, his voice low, threatening.

The brave smiled suddenly and yanked his horse back—evidently impressed at Fargo's forthright response.

"Will you tell these Crows to back off, Crow Woman?" Fargo told her.

"Why?" she said. "You do fine."

"Are these your people?"

"I do not know. But soon we—"

Then she let out a very unladylike cry, left Fargo, and darted between two horsemen so swiftly one of the ponies reared skittishly. Her objective was a Crow brave who had just ridden into the clearing. At sight of Crow Woman the brave swung himself off his horse in that easy, careless way Indians had, and ran to meet her.

Still shrieking, Crow Woman embraced the brave, and as soon as Fargo got a better look at him, he saw the family resemblance. At the very least Crow Woman had found a brother.

This loosened things up a bit. At once the other braves swung from their ponies, some rushing to greet Crow Woman, others crowding around

Fargo, their eager copper hands stroking the handsome Ovaro. Fargo kept a firm grip on his pinto's bridle.

Before long, speaking in Crow dialect at an astonishing rate, Crow Woman proceeded to tell the Crows crowding around her about Fargo and herself—and much else besides, Fargo had no doubt. The upshot of it was that Fargo and Crow Woman went back to their camp so there could be a feast and a night of dancing to celebrate the return of Nat-ah-Tahnee, as Crow Woman was known among her own people. Later that night— much later—Crow Woman told Fargo what it meant: Night Eyes.

The next morning, Fargo's head reeling still from the pounding of drums and his stomach distended from the bowls of boiled dog meat that he had eaten, he emerged from his lodge with Crow Woman—and found a magnificent Indian cavalry, armed and eager for battle, at his service.

When he climbed onto his already saddled Ovaro, he looked back at Crow Woman. She watched him from the entrance to the lodge where they had spent the night, her almond-shaped eyes glowing. He would sure as hell miss her, he realized with a sudden pang—especially when he thought of how she had put him to sleep finally the night before, despite all that drumming.

Crow Woman's brother, Kicking Deer, was the leader of the war party, and Fargo guessed Crow Woman had told him much about Fargo—and most of what she had told him must have been impressive, considering the deference and respect Kicking Deer and the other Crow warriors showed him. The result was that Fargo was allowed to act as second in command to Kicking Deer.

In less than two days, they made it back to the wagons, riding night and day, stopping only to rest and feed the horses. Late on a sweltering afternoon they rode in sight of the escarpment and heard the first faint pop of distant gunfire.

The Indians at once pulled their mounts to a halt and dismounted. Appalled, Fargo swung his pinto around and was preparing to harangue them angrily when he saw what the Crow warriors were doing. They were seeing to their ancient rifles, their knives, lances, and bows—and once that was taken care of, they proceeded to paint their faces.

Fargo took a deep breath to contain his impatience, and saw to the load in his Colt. Then he checked the firing pin on his Sharps. Yet still the Sioux were busy with their preparations. In a fever of impatience, Fargo masked his irritation by honing to a razor-sharp edge the blade of his bowie.

At last the Sioux mounted up and were ready to move on.

As Fargo swung into his saddle, Kicking Deer nudged his pony alongside Fargo's. He had Crow Woman's long face, high cheekbones, and handsome eyes. He could not have been more than thirty, but his broad shoulders were already pocked and puckered with the scars of countless battles. He smiled at Fargo, revealing brilliantly white teeth.

"Skye Fargo go first, Crow follow."

This, Fargo realized, was an honor. For this one brief sortie, Skye Fargo, a white man, was going to lead a war party of Crow into battle against their ancient enemy, the Sioux.

Fargo nodded, turned the pinto, and spurred it forward, the Crow following him in a broad line. Topping a low ridge, Fargo saw ahead of him the steep slope and above it the ledge. Just before him on the flat leading to the slope was the Sioux camp, a large herd of ponies grazing off to his right. Three braves were sitting about the fire, a few were working on their weapons, others seemed to be resting, while most of these Indians appeared to be wounded slightly.

As Fargo charged the camp, he saw smoke pumping from the ledge, coming from the direction of the wagons. Cursing, Fargo spurred his pinto to greater speed, sweeping directly through the camp as he headed for the slope. Behind Fargo, the Crow let loose with their war cries. Ahead of Fargo the startled Sioux grabbed up their weapons and prepared to defend themselves.

One old Sioux sitting cross-legged by the fire threw off the bloodstained blanket he had wrapped around his torn body and lunged up at Fargo with his lance. Fargo parried the lance with his Colt barrel and fired down into the old warrior's chest. The old man's face expressed almost sweet resignation as he reeled back and toppled to the ground—and in that instant Fargo recognized the warrior.

It was Chief Black Feather.

Fargo did not slow down. He kept going, reached the slope, and swept on up it toward the burning wagons. No Sioux were in sight on the slope or on the ridge. This alarmed Fargo. He glanced back. The Crow warriors had seemingly left no one alive as they swept through the Sioux camp after Fargo.

Reaching the crest of the ridge, Fargo was met by two Sioux. One of them fired hastily up at him with a rifle and missed; the other had an ancient pistol that misfired. Fargo swept on past them, leaving them to the Crows. Rounding a boulder, he came in sight of the wagons and saw the canvas on one of them blazing. The attacking Sioux clustered about both wagons like bees on a hive.

Fargo began using his Colt. Two Sioux went down; others went for cover. When the hammer snapped down on an empty chamber, Fargo yanked his Sharps out of its scabbard and fired into a brave standing transfixed on a wagon seat.

Fargo reached the wagons and found himself in the midst of the attacking Sioux. Flinging himself off his pinto, he tackled a big painted warrior who was busy slashing a hole in a wagon canvas. They slammed to the ground and began attempting to throttle each other at the feet of the astonished Sioux. The Sioux warrior managed to break free and was slithering frantically away from Fargo when a Crow horseman galloped over his head, shattering it like a pumpkin.

Suddenly the Crow warriors were at his side, flailing away with their war clubs and hatchets. Instantly, what had been a queer, one-sided battle with Fargo on the short end became a rout with his enemies in flight. Jumping to his feet, Fargo drew his empty Colt and, using it as a club, began laying furiously about him. The feel of Sioux bone crunching under his blows felt sweet indeed as he reminded himself of what must lay inside the shattered wagons.

Standing happily alongside Fargo, the Crows joined Fargo and clubbed and knifed down the surprised Sioux. A few Sioux ran for cover, which only gave those Crows who had not yet counted coup a chance to overtake and scalp them—a game they relished.

The battle was over almost as completely as it had begun. Kicking aside a dead Sioux, Fargo climbed up into the seat of the first wagon and peered into it. He had expected to find clubbed and bleeding bodies, the women huddled together in mute horror. He found nothing. Only a few empty water barrels, trunks, and leather gear. Jumping down, he raced to the other wagon. The blazing canvas had been ripped off the frames by the Crow, and again, peering over the sides, he found that the attacking Sioux had been swarming over empty wagons.

"Hey, down there!"

The voice came from almost directly overhead.

Fargo took a step back from the wagons and glanced up.

"Who's up there?" cried Fargo.

"That you, Fargo?" came Jeb's voice. " 'Bout time you got here!"

And then Fargo saw Jeb and Matthew's face peering down at him from a cleft high in the rock face. A moment later Tyler's face peered down as well.

"Where's the others?"

"Right here behind us!"

"How the hell did you get up there?"

"We climbed, you son of a bitch. What'd you think? We flew?"

"Get on down here!"

"That won't be so easy. Give us time."

Fargo grinned and shook his head. Then he looked about him at his Crow allies. Most of the war party had ridden off after fleeing Sioux, but Kicking Deer was approaching, bloody scalps dangling from his belt. He smiled at Fargo and pointed up at the cleft.

"Your people all alive?" he asked.

"That's right," said Fargo, unable to keep the elation he felt out of his voice. "So far. Now all they have to do is climb down."

The operation was much simpler than it had at first appeared. Directing things from above and using ropes, Jeb saw to it that everyone was safely down before he clambered down himself, making the descent as swiftly as a goat—an old goat.

Fargo had already greeted the others. Sam and Beth were subdued and wary as they stared up at

147

the fierce, grotesquely Painted Crow warriors as they rode up on their prancing horses. Angelique and Theresa were also somewhat nervous, but Tyler and Matthew, weary and bloodstained, seemed very pleased to welcome Kicking Deer and the other Crows with him. Except for the two children, all five of them appeared to have sustained minor wounds. A bloody bandage was wrapped around Tyler's head, but he seemed none the worse for it as he stationed himself close beside Theresa and the two children.

"Didn't know you were part mountain," Fargo told Jeb as he strode forward to greet the old hunter.

The two shook hands heartily. Jeb's eyes gleamed in triumph. "I told you I'd be here waitin' for you when you got back. No matter how long it took."

"Sorry it took so long."

"I wasn't worried."

"Not much, you weren't."

"Well," the old man drawled, "toward the end there, this here scalp of mine did begin to crawl some."

Fargo laughed and they turned to join the others.

"I like your Indian cavalry," Jeb said, noting the brilliantly plumed warriors astride their ponies who were drifting back now to the wagons, most of them with fresh, dripping trophies, and all of them pulling behind them Sioux horseflesh. Fargo recognized the chief's pony, and the others he had taken from the Blackfoot war party.

"Damn fine bunch of fighters," Fargo acknowledged. "They've promised to escort us to Fort Laramie."

"Not painted like that, I hope."

Fargo laughed.

"Well, before they do, I would sure like 'em to nail Black Feather. I won't feel safe until that son of a bitch is walking around without his hair. I never saw such a persistent old bastard."

"He's dead."

"You sure of that?"

"I killed him riding through his camp. He looked old and beat-up, like he realized he had made a mistake and was hoping for an end to it. I think I did him a favor."

"Well, maybe you did, boss. You sure as hell did us one."

They reached the rest of the party then and took a good long time greeting each other, since Fargo had to introduce all of them to Kicking Deer, who in turn felt obliged to introduce his lieutenants. The children were the instant favorites of the Crows, and before long Sam and Beth had shed their shyness enough to allow the Indians to lift and carry them about on their backs.

They made camp that night some distance from where the Sioux had camped, and with plenty of Crow posted as sentries, the entire party was promised a chance finally to sleep uninterrupted throughout the night. Fargo did not fail to notice that it was with Jeb that Angelique moved off when it came time to selecting places to sleep, while Tyler kept close to Theresa and the two children.

Fargo was almost asleep whem Matthew Wayland approached him. Fargo sat up and greeted the old man. He looked chipper, his eyes alert, almost as if the recent troubles had given him a new lease on life.

"I have been meaning to approach you before this," he said somewhat nervously. "You didn't mention Crow Woman. I was wondering. She is all right now, is she?"

"She's with her people. That feller Kicking Deer is her brother."

Matthew sighed. "I am glad."

"You liked her, did you?"

In the darkness Fargo could not be sure, but he thought the old man blushed. "Yes, very much. She was . . . patient with me. And warm."

"You ain't goin' to get no argument from me on that. She was all woman."

"If you see her again, give her my regards."

"That ain't likely—that I'll see her again, I mean—but if I do, I will be glad to convey your respects."

"That is very decent of you, Fargo."

Matthew started to leave, then looked back at Fargo. "How soon do you think we'll be able to push on to Fort Laramie?"

"As soon as we shoot some fresh meat and get the wagons repaired. Shouldn't take more'n a day or two."

"Fine."

The old man turned and moved off. Watching

him go, Fargo wondered if maybe he couldn't manufacture some kind of excuse so he could convey Matthew Wayland's respects to Crow Woman in person.

Then he chided himself for entertaining such a nonsensical idea and scooted deeper into his sleeping bag. He had a long journey to Fort Laramie still ahead of him and it would go a whole hell of a lot faster if he could finally get some sleep at night.

Still, before Fargo dropped off, he could almost feel the savage pull of Crow Woman's lips on his . . .

10

They arrived at Fort Laramie a week later.

Fargo rode ahead of the small, battered wagon train, with Jeb, Kicking Deer, and another Crow brave, Beaver Tail, at his side. Behind them came Angelique driving Jeb's wagon and then Theresa Wayland's wagon, her father on the seat beside her with the heads of Sam and Beth peeking out between them. Tyler rode close alongside. On Fargo's advice he was no longer wearing his army tunic or trousers. Instead, he was wearing an extra buckskin shirt of Fargo's along with a pair of his buckskin trousers.

The two sentires at the entrance to the post challenged Fargo and his two Crow companions, but Fargo explained matters quickly to the private and inquired the whereabouts of the commanding officer's headquarters, even though he knew perfectly well where it was.

He was given directions courteously and his small party was allowed to proceed into the fort. Though there were no Indian tepees set up inside the fort itself, there were many just outside, and on the grounds of the fort there wandered Indians of every description. Many of them were not a pleasant sight. Too many of the squaws were squalid whores plying their trade with the desperate connivance of their pathetic, drunken husbands. As Fargo and many of his companions had said often enough: in the end, it would not be the settlers or the army that would kill off the Indians, but the rum.

There was a sharp difference between the appeaance of those Indians milling about inside the fort and the proud Crow warriors who rode beside Fargo and Jeb, and neither man missed noting the contempt with which Kicking Deer and Beaver Tail gazed upon these blanket Indians.

Pulling up a hundred yards or so from the entrance, Fargo waved Tyler closer. Tyler spurred away from Theresa's wagon and joined them.

"What does Theresa want to do?" Fargo asked him.

Tyler grinned and pointed to a long train of Conestoga wagons on the far side of the fort. "She saw them wagons first thing. 'Settlers,' she cried. I guess we'll head over there."

Fargo nodded. "All right. We'll join you later when we get the chance."

Tyler rode back to Theresa's wagon and soon it

turned toward the Conestogas, Tyler riding close alongside. Theresa, Matthew, and the children waved to Fargo and the others as they drove off.

Angelique called up to Jeb then. "Where we headed, Jeb?"

Jeb saw a cluster of wagons close by the sutler's store. "Over there," he told her. "I'll join you."

She nodded and headed in that direction.

Jeb glanced at Fargo. "Now, what, Fargo? You goin' in to see this here commanding officer?"

"I ought to pay my respects."

"That's the right and proper thing to do, all right. But do you think you should?"

Fargo laughed. "Don't worry. I'm not going to say anything about Tyler."

"Hell. I know that. But that ain't what's botherin' me. How you goin' to explain Kicking Deer and Beaver Tail, and what happened out there?"

"You let me handle that."

"I don't like it."

"We got to explain our presence and these two wagons or we'll only cause Tyler trouble. We can't duck in here like outlaws. Meet me at the trading post in about half an hour while I test this here commanding officer's brand of whiskey."

With a sigh, Jeb nodded. He and the two Indians peeled off, heading toward the sutler's store. Fargo rode straight for the headquarters building. He shared Jeb's misgivings, but there was a certain protocol that had to be followed when entering an army post, and Fargo knew that it would complicate matters if he ignored that fact.

Already, he was sure, news of his arrival, including the two Crow warriors, had reached the major in command.

The major's name was Thompson Willoughby, a solid, broad-shouldered man no more than five and a half feet tall. His face was solid, his jaw square. But Fargo did not particularly like his eyes, and his voice held a heartiness that Fargo sensed the major didn't feel. Ever.

He welcomed Fargo into his office with bluff cordiality and offered him a drink. A small drink. Whiskey. And he diluted it with water.

"Sit down! Sit down," Willoughby cried as soon as he had handed Fargo his glass. "I see you rode in here with a handsome escort. Crows! In full war regalia."

Fargo sat down and nodded. "They're friendlies, Major."

"I should hope so. If they weren't, I would have had them clapped in irons the moment they entered this fort. The Crows protest their love of white men, Mister Fargo, but they are savages all the same, vicious children that would bully and kill the first chance they get. I prefer the more straightforward aborigines, the Blackfeet. They made no pretense of being friendly with settlers or whites of any stripe."

"They are a mean lot, and that's the truth," Fargo admitted.

The major smiled. "I noticed one of your wagons has felt the torch of hostile forces."

"Yes."

"Sioux?"

Fargo smiled.

"But you managed to outrun them?"

"With the help of those Crows you saw with me."

"Ah, yes. They are the traditional foes of the Sioux, aren't they?"

Fargo took a sip of his watered whiskey. "Yep. Say, Major, you wouldn't happen to know if Major Hollister is close by?"

"He and his men are on their way east," the major sighed, "to fight in that fool war. But I shouldn't worry. It'll be over in a few months. The rebels will be quickly routed."

"I am sure."

"Well, then, Mister Fargo, welcome to Fort Laramie. If there is anything I can do to make your stay a pleasant one, please be sure to let me know. I will hold you responsible for the behavior of your two aborigines, however. Do you mind telling me why they have come this far with you?"

"To trade. They have some fine pelts."

Maj. Willoughby got to his feet and tossed down the rest of his whiskey. "Thank you, Mister Fargo, it has been a pleasure meeting you."

Fargo got up and started from the room without bothering to finish the whiskey. He was almost to the door when Willoughby cleared his throat.

"Mister Fargo . . . ?"

Fargo halted and turned.

"Did you by any chance get wind of a large band of troopers that had taken over Major Hollister's fort?"

"I heard about it."

"From whom?"

"The trappers in the region."

"So you kept away from the fort?"

"Yes."

"Then why did you ask about Major Hollister?"

"I thought I'd tell him what happened."

"Are you aware that a detachment of troops sent from here to bring those deserters in went over to them, murdering an officer in the process?"

"No, I didn't."

"Then you wouldn't mind if my adjutant, Captain Forman, were to look you up—get some idea of the situation out there, the mood of the tribes, that sort of thing."

"Not at all, Major."

"Good afternoon, Mister Fargo."

Fargo found Jeb at the sutler's store, sitting with Angelique at a table in the rear. Kicking Deer and Beaver Tail were sitting at an adjoining table. Both Indians were drinking a bottle of sarsaparilla rather than liquor, and they seemed profoundly uncomfortable sitting in this close, low-ceilinged annex to the store, the sound of heavy voices coming at them out of the thick, swirling cigar smoke. Angelique, too, seemed close to wincing.

"Let's get out of here," Fargo said as soon as he reached their tables.

The four nodded eagerly and left with Fargo. Outside in the fresh air, they all took a deep breath.

157

Kicking Deer turned to Fargo. "I go to wagon now, get pelts for trade. Then we go from this place."

"It stinks of the white man, don't it?" said Jeb, grinning at the tall Indian.

Kicking Deer fixed him with his black eyes, then nodded. Emphatically. Jeb's was not an idle comment as far as Kicking Deer was concerned.

"I'd better go with them," Angelique said.

"Good idea," said Jeb.

"We'll wait here," Fargo said.

The three started for Angelique's wagon.

On their trip to the fort, Kicking Deer had left them to ride back to his village to pick up the pelts he had stored so that he could make this journey to the trading post. In the company of Beaver Tail, he had overtaken them the day before. Kicking Deer had not wanted to come to the fort earlier to trade because of the trouble he was afraid would erupt if he were to appear at this army fort, not as a blanket Indian, but as a free Crow warrior, one who still rode and fought as his forefathers had.

All this Kicking Deer had made clear to Fargo as they neared the fort, and Fargo had understood. Fargo's hope now was that nothing would happen to mar this trip to the fort for Kicking Deer and his companion. Kicking Deer had spoken to him with gleaming eyes of the many fine things he would bring back to his woman—the beads, the warm blankets, and especially the iron pots and other cooking utensils.

"I don't like this major," Fargo said.

"Why not?"

"I don't trust him."

"What'd you tell him?"

"He was a fool. He told me. I just listened and nodded. He knows just enough of this country to know nothing."

"I have seen that kind before."

"He knows about the renegade troopers and that they took over Fort Alexander. Seems a detachment from here was sent to bring Blaine and his men in, but ended up joining Blaine instead. The major's sending his adjutant to question me some more."

Jeb swore. "Tyler ain't told us, but I'll bet he was a member of that detachment."

"Got sucked in, more than likely."

"That's the way I see it."

"It took courage to come back here."

"No. Not courage. The damn fool's in love."

"He'll just have to keep out of sight."

"If he knows what's good for him."

Kicking Deer and Beaver Tail returned with their pelts. Each Indian carried a large bale on his shoulder. They went around to the rear of the sutler's store and through another entrance that led to the trading post. Five men were sitting around an unlit potbellied stove, whiskey jugs sitting on the floor beside them. The place smelled of unwashed feet and cheap cigars.

The men around the stove were joshing with the owner of the trading post, who was standing inside the wire-mesh enclosure. He was a tall, balding individual, with cold, shrewd eyes. When he saw the two Indians lugging in the pelts, he broke off with the five men and hurried over to the counter.

Fargo and Jeb stood to one side as the Indians unpacked their furs and showed them to the owner. He didn't ask the names of the Indians and he didn't introduce himself. Fargo was immediately impressed by the quality of the furs Kicking Deer had brought. There were beaver pelts, otter and bear pelts, all of them well cleaned, with not a mark on them. Prime furs.

The bargain for goods in payment was short and abrupt. The owner took the furs, inspected them closely, placed them to one side, then selected two thin, moth-eaten blankets, a box of cheap trinkets, and a small kitchen knife, and shoved them across the counter to Kicking Deer.

Fargo and Jeb were as astounded as the two Indians.

"Hey, wait a minute there," Fargo said. "What you just shoved over there ain't worth one of them pelts."

Startled, the owner looked at Fargo. "Oh, I'm sorry, sir. Are these your pelts?"

"What's that go to do with it?"

"Well, I didn't realize. By all means, select what you think they are worth. I thought these pelts belonged to these savages."

"They do," Fargo said.

"But we'll still pick out what we think they're worth," finished Jeb.

"Now, just a minute," the owner cried.

Fargo reached over and grabbed the man by his shirt collar and dragged him halfway across the counter. "Now, you listen, and listen good. These here Crow Indians are my friends. You'll give them what these furs deserve or I'll wipe this floor up with your face, *then* I'll take what the furs are worth! That clear enough for you?"

Fargo suddenly felt a strong hand clamp down on his shoulder and then yank back. He spun around swinging, and in a second it was the four of them—the two Indians, Jeb, and Fargo— against five loungers. For a while it sounded like they were shoeing a bronc in the room's narrow confines, but the fight was brief and at its conclusion, the five loungers were on the floor, only one of them conscious enough to shake his head and spit out what teeth he had left.

Fargo turned to the owner. "Now," he said, "trade!"

Fargo was helping the two Indians pack their goods in Jeb's wagon when the detail of troopers, armed and primed for action, surrounded the wagon.

The shavetail in charge of the four troopers looked nervous enough to shoot off his foot if he had to go for his weapon, and the troopers backing him looked just as unsettled.

"Easy, Lieutenant," Fargo said, walking slowly toward the young officer. "What's this all about?"

"Them two Indians, sir. The sutler says they stole those goods you're packin'."

"They didn't steal them. They traded for them."

"Beggin' your pardon, sir, but I have my orders. They are to come with me."

"With you?"

"Yes, sir. To the guardhouse."

"This is crazy. They ain't done nothin'."

"Yes, sir. But I have my orders."

"Damn your orders!"

"I can't do that, sir."

"And stop callin' me sir! I was in that tradin' post. I'm as much to blame as these two Indians."

"Yes, sir, but I am supposed to take the Indians with me."

"Who gave the order?"

"The major, sir."

Fargo swung around to Kicking Deer and Beaver Tail. "I'll go see the major," he told them. "He can't keep you. I'll see to it."

The two Indians looked at him. "I do not think this major like the Crow. But I will do as you say."

At that moment Jeb and Tyler ran up.

"What the hell's going on?" Jeb wanted to know.

Fargo explained it to them.

Furious, Jeb walked up to the lieutenant. "Listen, sonny, you get yourself and your damned bluecoats the hell out of here! This here's my wagon and these here Indians are my friends!"

The lieutenant swallowed unhappily, then happened to glance in Tyler's direction. Tyler nervously returned his gaze. Fargo saw the lieutenant's face grow cold and what little resolve he had left flowed suddenly back into it.

"I must insist," the lieutenant said, his voice

rising slightly. "There will be trouble if you do not allow these Indians to be taken peaceably to the guardhouse."

Fargo stepped closer to Jeb and pulled him back. "All right, Lieutenant," he told the youngster, "go ahead."

The lieutenant ordered his men to take the Indians into custody. They formed a neat triangle around Kicking Deer and Beaver Tail and marched off.

Fargo glanced at Tyler. "You know that lieutenant?"

"I know him."

"Do you think he recognized you?"

"If he did, I'm in the soup. He knows I was with that detachment that joined Blaine's group."

"You didn't tell us about that, Tyler."

"It's an ugly story. I went along because if I didn't I would have died the same way the lieutenant with us did. By hanging."

"They strung him up?"

"He was a rotten officer, Fargo. But he didn't deserve to die like that."

"You'll have to pull out of here—now."

"I can't."

"Why the hell not?"

"Theresa and I are joining this wagon train. It's pulling out tomorrow, heading for California. There's a minister on the wagon train. He says he'll marry us."

"Go back to her, then, and lay low."

As Tyler hurried off, Jeb turned to Fargo. "Now what?"

"We go explain things to that major."

The major listened politely to what Fargo and Jeb had to say about the disagreement at the trading post, not hesitating to emphasize their own contribution. When they had finished, the major went to his door, opened it, and called his adjutant into his office.

At once the adjutant strode in. The major introduced him as Capt. Forman. The captain carried himself as erect as a ramrod, and his thinning hair was combed straight back, each strand shining brightly from the Macassar oil he dumped on it.

The major handled the introductions, then leaned back in his chair to allow his adjutant to speak.

"Gentlemen," said the captain, still standing, "do you realize you have been harboring a fugitive?"

"A fugitive?"

"A private Tyler, I believe. He was spotted by Lieutenant Campbell within this past hour."

"A fugitive?"

"One of those men who were sent to bring in Blaine and his deserters. Don't deny it. He is already in custody—along with your two murderous Crow chieftains."

"Murderous Crow chieftains?" Fargo cried. "What the hell are you talking about, Captain? I just got through telling the major here what happened in that trading post. And we didn't kill anybody."

The major stood up, his eyes blazing. "That's enough, from both of you. I've heard all I need to hear. You two men will have until tomorrow to quit this post. If you remain after eight A.M., you will join Tyler and those two savages in the guardhouse. Is that clear?"

"On what charges?" Fargo demanded.

"For giving aid and comfort to the enemies of this country and for aiding and abetting the escape of an army deserter and possible murderer. You see, gentlemen, we know not only about this Tyler, but also about Kicking Deer and his brother assassin, Beaver Tail. Those furs your Indian friends brought in for trade this afternoon were taken from a scalped and mutilated fur trapper found dead not one hundred miles from here."

"You got proof of that?"

"One of those men you assaulted this afternoon was this same fur trapper's partner. He recognized the pelts as soon as the Indian began showing them."

"That's a lie!"

"Perhaps, but it will stand up in court—and help us rid the frontier of two more insolent aborigines."

Jeb started to protest, but Fargo grabbed him by the arm and pulled him from the room. There was no sense arguing with the military, not when they had all the cards.

11

On a bright Monday morning three weeks later, an army ambulance left Fort Laramie and started on the trail south. Inside, in shackles, were Kicking Deer, Beaver Tail, and Tyler. The two Indians were heading for a Kiowa agency less than a hundred miles south, but Tyler's destination was much farther: Leavenworth, Kansas.

Sitting beside the driver of the team was Corp. Riley, a shotgun across his lap. Riding drag on the ambulance were two troopers, privates. All four soldiers were pleased at this chance to get the hell out of Fort Laramie and kick up their heels at the towns they passed through—and all at government expense.

Ten miles south of the fort, the trail wound between high, rounded hills, the tops of which were occasionally spiked with scrub pine. The landscape was dry, the wind hot, and inside the ambulance it was stifling. The leather side curtains had been rolled up, but that only served to expose the three prisoners to the hot wind and the blistering sunlight.

The driver of the team, mopping his brow and cursing silently as he glanced up at the blistering sun, was forced to slow constantly as he negotiated the curving, rutted trail. By now the deep ruts formed in the spring and early summer had been baked to the consistency of stone. The ambulance was taking considerable punishment.

Riley glanced back at the prisoners. They appeared to be in some discomfort due to the heat and their shackles as they struggled to remain seated on their wooden benches.

"Slow down," the corporal said to the driver. "We ain't in no hurry."

"Maybe not, but I'd sure as hell like to get out of this heat. I wish we could find a place with some shade so we could pull up."

"There's a town ten miles ahead. We should be there by noon."

"Not if we slow down."

"We won't get there at all if we lose a wheel."

The private shrugged and slowed the two horses. A second later, they hit a spectacular rut. The wagon lifted, then came down crookedly. There was a loud snap, like a gunshot, and the wagon suddenly lurched back and to the right.

"It's an axle," the driver cried. "The rear axle!" He sawed back on the reins to bring the horses to a halt, then climbed down and hurried to the rear of the ambulance, Corp. Riley at his side.

The right rear of the wagon was resting on the ground, the wheel lying flat alongside the trail. The axle had evidently broken within inches of the spoked wheel. The driver got down on his hands and knees to find the exact spot where the axle had given way.

He found it; then, reaching in under the wagon bed to feel of it, he swore loudly and jumped up. "Goddamm it! It's been sawed through—most of it, anyway!"

"Sawed through?"

The driver nodded grimly. "Not all the way, but enough to weaken it."

By then the two drag riders had dismounted and were approaching, leading their horses. They looked as unhappy as Riley and the driver.

"We got to go back, Corporal?" one of them asked. It was obvious the prospect was a bleak one.

"We got no axle," the driver replied. "What else can we do?"

Riley looked around at the hills, frowning. "Maybe we could cut one of them trees up there and make a fresh axle."

"What would we cut down a tree with, Corporal?" demanded the driver.

"Sorry," the corporal said. "It was just an idea."

"Can we be of any assistance?"

The four troopers turned to see two masked riders approaching, their big six-guns trained on them.

"Oh, shit," said the driver.

"Drop the shotgun, Corporal," said the closest rider as he thumb-cocked his Colt.

The corporal did as he was told.

Fargo was not riding his Ovaro, nor was he wearing his buckskins or hat, and he was careful to keep the kerchief high on the bridge of his nose as he and Jeb rode closer. As soon as the corporal dropped the shotgun, Fargo dismounted and kicked it well off the road. Then he disarmed the remaining troopers.

"Where's the keys to the shackles?" Fargo asked the corporal.

"I ain't tellin' you."

"That's a fool way to behave. We know the keys are on you. Somewhere. We'll find them even if we have to hang you by your ankles."

The corporal reached into a rear pocket and handed Fargo the keys. Fargo tossed them to Jeb, who quickly climbed into the wagon to free the prisoners.

As Jeb tended to this, Fargo had the troopers unsaddle the two army horses, then release the team from their traces and take off their collars. When this had been accomplished, Fargo fired a shot close behind them. The four horses bolted and a moment later disappeared beyond the next turn.

By this time the prisoners had been freed and were standing woozily alongside Jeb. Fargo joined them and turned to the four troopers.

"Fort Laramie is a good day's walk from here," he told them. "It won't be pleasant in those boots.

We suggest you take cover during the day and travel only at night."

"There's a stream due south of here about two miles," Jeb said. "There's also canteens and a cache of food near it. You shouldn't have no trouble finding them."

"We'll need our guns," said the corporal.

"Yeah," Fargo acknowledged. "When we reach the top of that hill up there, we'll throw your handguns and the shotgun down to you."

"Thanks."

"You don't seem very upset, Corporal," Fargo remarked.

"We know all about this here business with the Crows and Tyler," the trooper said. "Hell, if it wasn't against regulations, we'd wish you luck."

"Thank you, Corporal. And good luck to you."

In a shaded gulley not far from where the army ambulance broke down, Fargo's pinto and two other horses were waiting. The transfer of horses was made swiftly, and by nightfall the five men had arrived at the high, wooded valley where Angelique was waiting with Jeb's wagon.

Angelique soon had a fire going and hot food in their stomachs. Afterward, Jeb passed around a bottle of very good whiskey. Kicking Deer and Beaver Tail took only cautious sips at first, but soon their manner brightened as it became clear to them that they were really free men once more.

It was getting late. Jeb turned to Tyler.

"Ever hear of a place called Monterey?"

"Nope."

"It's in California, along the coast south of San

Francisco. I been there once. I'm goin' back there now—with Angelique. I figure I've worn out my welcome in these parts."

"More power to you," said Tyler gloomily.

"Angelique and me, we wondered if you might want to come along with us."

"I don't know, Jeb. I got to think on it."

"Well, while yer doin' that, read this here that Miss Theresa left for you." As Jeb spoke, he pulled a crumpled letter out of his pocket and handed it to Tyler. "I understand it was Monterey she and her father was headin' to with them two young'uns when they pulled out with that wagon train."

As Tyler snatched the letter from Jeb and ripped it open, Fargo, smiling, said to him, "Why don't you go over to the wagon and light a lamp so you can read it in private?"

"Sure," Tyler managed, getting to his feet and making a beeline for the wagon.

As they watched him go, there were smiles all around—except for the two Indians, who were not quite sure what was going on.

Fargo turned to Kicking Deer. "Look, like Tyler's goin' to California. What about you two gents?"

Kicking Deer straightened his back. "We return to our people. Let the bluecoats come after us."

"I wouldn't worry none about that," Jeb said. "I been hearing things while I hung around the post. That major and his adjutant ain't been handling things right with the Indians. Word is he's bein' sent back East soon to deal with that rebel uprisin', the one he's so sure won't last another week or so. I doubt if he'll be back."

"Another thing," Fargo said. "Everyone at the fort knows what really happened in that trader's shop. And that includes the brass in Washington."

"Then why we get sent to agency?" Kicking Deer demanded.

"It's one thing for the army to know it's done a fool thing—it's something else for it to admit it openly. They had to go along with the major, but that don't mean they like it. The major put them in a real embarrassing position."

"I do not understand," said Kicking Deer. "If they know it is wrong, why they not let us go?"

Fargo sighed. "I just told you."

"Never mind," Jeb said. "There ain't no way a sane man could understand the workin's of the military mind."

Fargo nodded in weary agreement, stood up, and stretched. He was suddenly very tired. He and Jeb had spent most of the previous evening under the four army ambulances parked at the fort, sawing away at the rear axles. They had known when and on what day Jeb and the two Indians were being sent south, but they had no idea which wagon the army would select for transporting them.

There were going to be a lot of surprises for those who used the wagons in the days ahead.

As Fargo was smoothing down his bedroll in a corner of the meadow sometime later, Angelique appeared out of the night and ran lightly over to him. Kneeling beside him, she smiled warmly.

"Jeb and I will be pulling out first thing in the morning, Fargo."

"I figured that," Fargo said.

"I will miss you," she said.

"Jeb's a fine man, as tough as nails, with a heart as big as this sky overhead."

"I know that. I'm goin' to be fine. But what about you, Fargo?"

"I got something I have to finish."

She nodded. "I knew that. And that means there's no place in your life for a woman."

"Not for any length of time, Angelique. I can't settle down. Not now. Not until I finish what I got to do."

Angelique nodded. "That's what Jeb told me. And I could see it myself in them lake-blue eyes of yours."

"I guess Jeb knows me pretty well, at that."

She shook her hair back off her shoulders and sat back. "He's thinking of doing some farming when we reach California. He says there's need for food now them gold seekers've settled in to stay. And he says the climate is just fine for his old bones."

"He's right. Or so I hear."

There was a silence after that, so quiet Fargo thought he could hear Angelique's heart beating. Suddenly she cleared her throat. "We had some good times, you and me, didn't we Fargo?"

"Sure as hell did."

"I'm going to kiss you good-bye now. So it'll be easier in the morning."

Without waiting for his response, she took his head in her hands and pulled his face close to hers. Her lips closed over his, then worked his mouth open, her tongue probing with all her old sensuality. Slipping arms around him, she held him so close that her could feel the heady warmth of her breasts as she crushed them against his chest. It was a kiss that stirred Fargo to his boot heels, and when it was over, Angelique jumped to her feet and vanished back into the night.

Leaving Fargo with a large problem.

The morning sun was just flooding the eastern sky when Jeb's wagon, with Tyler riding alongside, vanished beyond a distant ridge. Astride his Ovaro, Fargo turned to the two Crow Indians. They seemed as anxious to pull out as Jeb and Tyler had been. The night before, Jeb and Fargo had given the two Indians the goods they had traded for at the post. Their eyes were now gleaming with anticipation at the joy their treasures would bring when they arrived back at their lodges.

"Where Fargo go now?" Kicking Deer asked.

"North."

"Then you ride with us."

"For a while."

Kicking Deer smiled. "You stay with Kicking Deer's people."

Fargo hadn't given the possibility much thought. But he did need a chance to get rested up and get his bearings, flesh himself out some, and breathe air that was not contaminated with the stench of stable and saloon and sweaty, indoor bodies. The weeks of hanging around the post in various disguises while he and Jeb waited to make their move had not been pleasant.

At that moment the high bright uplands of the Rockies seemed to be just what he needed.

"Thanks, Kicking Deer. I might just do that."

The return of Kicking Deer and Beaver Tail to their people was something that Fargo realized he would never forget. Watching the joy on the faces of the old men and women and on the two young braves' squaws was more than enough reward for the chances he and Jeb had taken to free them. Fargo only wished that Jeb could have been there to witness it with him. The celebration lasted well into the night and was even more exhausting than Crow Woman's homecoming celebration.

And throughout it, Crow Woman remained an elusive figure who stayed just out of reach, watching as chief after chief spoke with Fargo and the eager young braves crowded around, all of them anxious to touch and know this astounding white god of the forest who could lead warriors into battle with such reckless bravery and yet, when it was all over, speak quietly and gently— then move on, always alone.

Such singleness of purpose awed them.

At last, as Fargo found himself being led to still another minor chieftain's lodge for yet another bowl of dog meat or venison, a hand reached out of the crush of bodies surrounding him, enclosed his wrist, and drew him around.

And he found himself looking into Crow Woman's dark, fathomless eyes.

Those braves crowding around understood. Swiftly, they melted away into the night.

"Now it is our time, Skye," Crow Woman told him, turning and leading him off to her lodge, one that was blessedly far from the leaping bonfire and the wild drums.

Pulling him into her lodge, she sat him down on a warm, fur-covered mat and proceeded to undress him. Warm water was waiting and she bathed him then, lovingly. When she had finished, she covered him with the fur of a great white wolf and snuggled under it with him.

"You are tired," she said. "Later, we will play—but now you sleep. The dawn will come and you will not need to leave this lodge. We will be together for as long as you want, until there is no more of you for me to take."

He smiled and rested his head on her silken breasts, the gentle prod of her nipples arousing him slightly, but not enough to chase the enormous fatigue that sat so heavily on his eyelids. So he did not fight it. As Crow Woman had just promised, there would be plenty of time for lovemaking in the days ahead.

With the hot lovely warmth of her body enclosing him, Fargo drifted off to sleep.

LOOKING FORWARD!
The following is the opening section
from the next novel in the exciting
Trailsman series from Signet:

The Trailsman #43
MESQUITE MANHUNT

1861—the New Mexico territory,
where the other word for savagery
was Apache . . .

Dammit, he should never have agreed to do it, the big man reprimanded himself as he inched his way alongside the jagged rocks. The full moon bathed the mesa in a silver light that outlined every sandstone pinnacle and butte as well as the six figures grouped around the small fire. They sat in the clear flatland, a dozen yards from the line of rocks that marched along one side of the mesa. Apache, of course, the big man muttered to himself. Their long, black, stringy hair, brow bands, and short-legged Indian ponies had told him that much. But he needed to know more, and once again he swore at himself for being there.

He inched forward again and felt the loose,

sandy soil dig into his naked abdomen. Except for B.V.D.s and his gun belt, he was stark-naked, his clothes back with the Ovaro where he'd left the horse on the other side of the line of rocks. He inched forward a little more and paused. A soft, warm wind blew across the mesa and he could hear the sound of the Apache talking in low, half-grunted sentences. Again, he edged forward along his belly and suddenly froze as he heard the loose sand move almost directly in front of him, the little pebbles not so much dislodged as rubbed against one another in a soft, slithering sound.

Shit, Fargo murmured inwardly as he watched the snake slip around the edge of a hedgehog cactus. The red, yellow, and black bands, unmistakable even in the pale light of the moon, marked it as a coral snake, as deadly as it was beautiful. A distant relative of the cobra, the coral snake was a nervous reptile. There'd be no coiling up before striking, no warning rattle, only an instant, darting flash that would make the red, yellow, and black into a blur of color.

Fargo's hand lay against his side, his fingertips touching the butt of the big Colt .45 in the holster. The snake slid forward, slowed, its forked tongue darting out to read the air. Fargo's lips pulled back in a tight grimace. If he had time to blow the snake away, the Apache would be on him in moments. The old saying fit too damn well, he grunted: he was between a rock and a hard place.

He watched through slitted eyes as the coral

snake slithered closer, moved only a half-foot from his bare shoulder, the forked tongue constantly darting out, detecting the heat of his body. Fargo's fingers closed around the butt of the big Colt. The deadly snake moved, its tongue flicking out almost too quickly to see, and suddenly, out of the corner of his eye, Fargo glimpsed the small, scurrying shape, tan on top, snowy white on the underside of its jaw, throat, and chest. He recognized the small, desert dweller as a white-throated wood rat, and he saw the snake suddenly change direction, slide across the ground with astonishing speed. The wood rat had given off a more concentrated area of heat and the serpent had fixed on it instantly. Fargo held motionless as he watched the coral snake disappear into the rocks after the rodent.

He let a sigh of relief blow through his lips in a slow hiss and he felt the wetness of his palms. Slowly, he wiped his hands along his legs and wrenched his attention back to the figures beside the fire. The six Apache continued to relax casually in the warm night, and grimacing, Fargo again inched his near-naked body over the dry, sandy soil. He kept to the edge of the jagged line of rocks. He'd have to leave their deep shadows to crawl closer along the open ground, he knew, but he'd wait till the Apache fell asleep. He halted, finally, pressed himself against the stones in the black shadows. He'd come as close as he dared without moving into the open, and he settled his powerfully muscled body into the shadows to wait, his chiseled handsomeness drawn tight.

He muttered silently at himself again and let his thoughts unwind backward. Old friends and old favors, that's why he was here, he growled inwardly, and his thoughts leapt back to the army post just north of the Rio Hondo, base of the Forty-first United States Cavalry Troop. The regiment was commanded by Maj. Thomas Carpenter, army career man, top-drawer field commander, and old friend. Tom Carpenter was the only reason he was here in the New Mexico Territory lying near-naked under a full moon trying to get too damn close to six Apaches.

He could've turned down Tom Carpenter, Fargo grimaced, but then he'd never been much for turning his back on old obligations. There was a time he'd never forget, when the major had backed him with half a regiment in an effort to box in one of the men he'd hunted to avenge the wiping out of his family. It seemed so long ago now and it had been the wrong man, but that didn't matter. What mattered was that Tom Carpenter had bent army regulations to help, had understood, had stuck his own neck out. And now he was the one in a bind and needing help. Besides, the major had offered three times the usual scout's pay, and it was a sin to turn down that kind of money. Fargo smiled wryly. That afternoon only a week ago in Tom Carpenter's office had been spent over a bottle of bourbon and a sack of memories.

But the reminiscences came to an end and the major had leaned forward, his long face even more drawn than usual, his graying hair somehow more gray. "Fargo, I'm like a damn cornstalk in the wind out here," he'd said. "I'm supposed to keep this whole New Mexico Territory in hand with one lousy regiment. You know what this place is, Fargo. The Spaniards couldn't handle it, the Mexicans were glad to get rid of it, and the Indians never gave it up. Now they want me to go find somebody the Apaches captured a month ago."

"That means somebody dead by now," Fargo had offered.

"Likely, but important people say maybe not. They want proof and I'm getting a lot of pressure," the major had said.

"Pressure? Important people?"

"Such as United States Senator Robert Talbot," the major said, and Fargo remembered his brows lifting. "The man he wants me to find is his brother, Dale Talbot." Fargo's brows had lifted further. "The senator and his party will be here next week," the major had gone on. "Of course, he doesn't know the first goddamn thing about this murderous, varmint-infested territory they're calling New Mexico. He thinks I'm going to wave a magic wand and have some answers for him. Hell, I know that's dam near impossible, but I've got to make a stab at it. I've got to show him I've tried. That's where you come in, Fargo. If there's anything to find, you can find it."

"Out of nowhere? I just pick a direction and start looking?" Fargo protested.

Tom Carpenter's laugh had been grim. "It's bad, but not that bad. Talbot had three men with him when the Apache hit. One, a boozy old guide named Johnny Kelter, managed to hide and stay alive. He told us where they hit Talbot. It's a jumping-off place for you. If you can just find out which Apaches took him, that'll be something I can wave at the good senator when he gets here, which will be next week sometime."

"That means you're giving me a week to get back with something," Fargo had said.

"I know, that's pretty impossible. Do the best you can, that's all," Tom Carpenter had said, and had given him the few facts he had. A handshake had been all that was needed after that, and Fargo thought about how he'd set off at once for the foot-hills of the Sacramento Mountains where Dale Talbot had been captured.

The Trailsman broke off his thoughts as one of the Apaches stood up, then another, and drew his attention back to them. As he watched, the six Indians stirred, changed positions as the fire burned low. They were preparing to bed down, he saw with grim satisfaction. He had picked up the six south of Cactus Creek and stayed well back until they'd halted for the night on the mesa. His plan was to put five of them out while they slept.

Hardly sporting, but the Apache would think nothing of slitting a man's throat while he slept. He needed only one awake to question. The Apache all spoke one or another dialect of the Athapaskan language, and he'd enough working familiarity with the tongue to serve him.

Fargo pushed himself up on one elbow as the Indians began to lie down in a half-circle around the embers of the little fire. They'd sleep quickly. Indians seldom tossed and turned. He let his gaze drift out across the mesa, travel along the black shadows of the line of rocks where he lay and, beyond the rocks, the foothills of the Sacramento Mountains touched by the moon's pale glow.

His eyes returned to the Indians. Two were still settling themselves, the others already turned on their sides to sleep. Suddenly, as he watched with an instant frown, all six of the Apache leapt to their feet with quick, catlike motions. He saw them freeze in place, listening, two with bone hunting knives drawn, their eyes searching the dark shadows of the rocks.

Goddamn, Fargo swore silently. He hadn't done anything to set them off, and the frown dug deeper into his forehead as he saw the Indians begin to move forward with cautious steps. With quick, silent, catlike movements, the six figures headed for the rocks. While he stared, they spread out and, as if galvanized into action, raced forward to the rocks only a few dozen yards from where he lay. He pushed himself up to a crouch, the big Colt .45 in his hand. What the hell had happened? he frowned into the night as he heard them scrambling up the rocks.

He strained his eyes, but the shadows were too deep for him to see anything, yet he heard one of the Apache shout, another answer, and then a woman's voice, a half-scream quickly drowned out by more triumphal shouts of the Apache.

Fargo stayed motionless and saw the Indians come into sight again, two dragging the figure between them while the others half-ran, half-leapt excitedly alongside. They reached the almost-burned-out fire and flung the woman to the ground. Fargo could see only a slender figure and long hair that hung loose and very blond even in the pale moonlight. The young woman got to her feet and aimed a sweeping blow at the nearest Indian; the Apache twisted away and brought a short left under the girl's swing. It caught her in the pit of the stomach and Fargo heard her gasp of pain as she fell to her knees. The Indian seized the long tresses and yanked, and the young woman went sprawling facedown on the ground.

Fargo felt his finger tighten on the trigger of the Colt, and he forced his hand to relax. Another of the Apache leapt atop the young woman as she lay on her stomach. He threw her skirt up over her waist and Fargo glimpsed the rounded, full rear under the pink bloomers the Indian started to rip down.

Damn, Fargo swore as his finger tightened on

the trigger again, but another Apache, a tall, lanky figure, seized the Indian atop the girl and yanked him off. Fargo heard his shout of command and the other Indian's angry answer as they faced each other. The others joined in and Fargo picked up the core of the argument. The lanky-figured one seemed to be the leader, and he ordered the girl to be brought back to their camp while the others were divided about enjoying her right there and then. But the lanky one was adamant. "No," Fargo heard him insist with authority. "We take her back first, let Huanco find out why she spy on us." Fargo heard the others grumble but the name of their chief seemed to have a quickly quieting effect as they backed down at once.

The lanky-figured Apache stepped to where the girl had pulled herself to her knees, and he motioned to one of the others. The man brought him a length of rawhide, and with rough, harsh motions he tied her wrists and ankles. With another piece of rawhide he made a leash from her wrists to his hand and moved away from the girl. Fargo saw him wrap the leather around his left wrist as he sat down on the ground. The Indian yanked hard and the girl pitched forward almost onto her face. "Lay down. Sleep," Fargo heard the Indian bark. The girl didn't need to know the language to get the message, and Fargo saw her stay on the ground, turn on her side, and grow quiet. The others had stretched out again and started to return to sleep, he saw, and as the soft night wind drifted across the mesa, Fargo had the answer to one question . . . but only one.

He peered at the young woman, watched her turn on her back and let the long, thick blond hair form a pillow under her head. Who was she? he frowned. More important, what the hell was she doing up in the rocks? Had she been lost, wandering around aimlessly? Or had she been watching the six Apache, too? He swore in silent anger. Who, why, or whatever, she had thoroughly ruined his chance to sneak up closer to the six Apache. He'd have to crawl across the open land and she'd be sure to see him as he neared. She'd make some move—out of surprise, if nothing else—and the one with the rawhide around his wrist would be awake instantly, the others only a half-second later, and he'd be caught on his belly out in the open. He'd nail some of them, but they were too spread out for him to get them all.

Damn her hide, Fargo swore as he sat back against the rocks and let thoughts pull at him. Not only had she wrecked his plans, but he couldn't see himself just leaving her to the Apache. Again he wondered where the hell she'd come from in the night. He angrily shook away speculation about her and forced his mind to pull at other avenues to save her hide and, hopefully, to get the answers he wanted from the Apache. The Indians fell asleep as Fargo let his thoughts continue to turn. He saw the girl move restlessly, and each time she did, the Indian with the rawhide on his wrist woke at once to yank hard in reprimand and she lay still.

As the moon began to slide down the far side of the night sky, Fargo pulled himself to his feet, his lips drawn back in a grimace. He'd come up with only one plan that had a chance of succeeding, and that counted on typical Apache behavior.

He began to pull himself up higher on the rocks at his back, climbing with the silent grace of a mountain cougar. Reaching the top of the rocks, he hunkered his near-naked frame between two tall rocks that let him look down on the Apaches and afforded him cover at the same time. That was all-important. If they saw him, they'd rush him no matter what kind of barrage he laid down. But they wouldn't rush him if he stayed unseen behind the rocks. The Apache didn't like the unknown. They wouldn't rush blindly at what they couldn't see or weren't reasonably certain about. It was their way, their own combination of bravery and prudence, cunning and caution.

He settled himself down and watched the first streaks of dawn spread across the sky. As the day began to lighten the dark, he took the Colt from its holster, rested it atop the rocks, and drew a bead on the sleeping figures below. He was poised and ready as the new day moved over the mesa and he saw the tall Apache wake first, get to his feet, and unwind the length of rawhide from his wrist. Fargo watched the young woman push herself up, and for the first time he had a proper look at her.

He saw a gray shirt pulled tight around a tall, slender figure, the long, thick hair wheat-gold in the new sun. He could make out a straight, thin nose and even features in an unquestionably attractive face. As the other Indians rose, one moved toward her and she instantly aimed a kick at him. He twisted away from the kick and caught her with a blow that hit her in the side. She grimaced, but her angry glare didn't change. Maybe she was afraid, but she was hard-nosed enough to tough it out, he noted.

Fargo leaned forward. The time had come. He aimed, let his finger slowly tighten on the trigger, a gentle pressure that would keep the Colt from bucking. The shot split the air and one of the Indians fell with a half-scream of pain, clutched at his leg with one hand as the others spun, their eyes searching the rocks.

Fargo called out in the Apache tongue. "Listen or you die," he said. "Many guns here." He watched the tall Apache scan the rocks with narrowed, probing black eyes. One of the others suddenly broke, raced for their ponies tethered to the side. Fargo fired again, no leg shot this time, and the Indian twisted, pitched forward, and lay still. Fargo saw the others remain frozen, their eyes on the rocks. "Bring the girl," he called. The others shot quick glances at the tall, lanky-figured one, who remained in a half-crouch. Fargo emphasized his words with a shot that sent a spray of dirt flying into the air at the edge of the Indian's right foot.

The Apache pushed the girl forward and followed her as she approached and halted at the base of the line of rocks. Fargo saw the Indian's black eyes darting back and forth up the jagged rocks as he tried to see through the narrow crevices in the stones. The Indian probably didn't buy the remark about many guns, Fargo realized, but he wasn't certain and, more important, the Apache knew he was an open target. "You take white man one moon ago," Fargo called from behind the rocks.

"No," the Indian grunted, and Fargo, peering from behind the narrow crevice, saw the girl frowning up at the rocks.

"You take white man, kill him," Fargo said, and the Indian shook his head again. Fargo fired a bullet that creased the brow band along the side of the Apache's head. The man flinched but his face remained set.

"No," the Indian repeated.

"You hear? You know?" Fargo asked.

The Indian shook his head again, his face a sullen mask.

Fargo grunted silently. He hadn't really expected an answer. If the Indian did know anything, he wouldn't be answering without a lot of pain and torture, but the questions had given him the time to study the man and he cursed softly. The Apache had no design on his moccasins, no necklace, no embroidered brow band, not even a beaded armband to mark him. But maybe that said something of itself, Fargo reflected. He lifted his voice again. "White Mountain?" he called, and saw the Apache nod. Fargo waited a long moment before he spoke again. "Leave the girl," he ordered, and saw the Apache peer intently up at the rocks. The Indian stayed, thoughts racing behind his angry black eyes. "Leave the girl," Fargo said again, and put more sharpness into his voice.

The Apache delayed another half-minute before he turned, deciding to leave with his skin intact. He walked slowly to the ponies and the others started to follow, the one limping along on his wounded leg. They dragged the dead one with them and draped him over one of the ponies, and Fargo saw the tall Apache mount a spotted pony and stare back at the rocks for a long moment. He was still trying to see a way to attack, and Fargo helped him make up his mind by firing a quick shot that whistled only inches over the Indian's head. The Apache turned his pony and galloped off across the mesa.

Fargo stayed in place and glanced down at the girl as she watched the Indians until they were out of sight. He waited and she turned to look up at the rocks, a frown across her brow. He saw very blue eyes that were as sharp as they were bright, full red lips under the straight nose, flat cheekbones, and a long, graceful neck that seemed terribly white against the wheat-colored hair. Modest breasts sat firmly under the gray shirt, he noted.

"Climb up here, honey," he called, then stood up and reloaded the Colt as he watched her pull her way slowly up the side of the rocks. He was waiting as she reached the top and leapt lightly down to the flat space beneath the jagged topline, and he saw her very blue eyes widen in surprise. She swept her glance up and down his powerfully muscled tall frame, the tight B.V.D.s, which left little to the imagination, and only the gun belt over them.

"Who are you, and what the hell were you doing up here in these rocks last night?" he asked.

Her eyes lingered on his crotch and then moved across his body again. "What the hell kind of an outfit is that?" she muttered.

"The kind of an outfit that just saved your little ass, honey," Fargo growled impatiently. "Start talking."

Her eyes flicked up and down his body again. "No," she said. "I'm not telling anything to anybody who goes around dressed like that."

JOIN THE *TRAILSMAN* READERS' PANEL

Help us bring you more of the books you like by filling out this survey and mailing it in today.

1. Book Title: _____

   Book #: _____

2. Using the scale below, how would you rate this book on the following features? Please write in one rating from 0-10 for each feature in the spaces provided.

POOR		NOT SO GOOD			O.K.			GOOD		EXCEL- LENT
0	1	2	3	4	5	6	7	8	9	10

RATING

Overall opinion of book .... _____
Plot/Story .... _____
Setting/Location .... _____
Writing Style .... _____
Character Development .... _____
Conclusion/Ending .... _____
Scene on Front Cover .... _____

3. About how many western books do you buy for yourself each month? _____

4. How would you classify yourself as a reader of westerns?
   I am a ( ) light ( ) medium ( ) heavy reader.

5. What is your education?
   ( ) High School (or less) ( ) 4 yrs. college
   ( ) 2 yrs. college ( ) Post Graduate

6. Age _____ 7. Sex: ( ) Male ( ) Female

Please Print Name_____

Address_____

City _____ State _____ Zip _____

Phone # ( )_____

Thank you. Please send to New American Library, Research Dept., 1633 Broadway, New York, NY 10019.